"*I wish I'd known you were going to be here....*"

"If I'd known *you* were going to be here I'd never have come!"

"Do you hate me so much, Tara?"

"As much as you hate me."

The silence stretched. Then the beautiful, spine-tingling voice spoke at last. "I never said I hated you."

She looked up, her eyes holding Sholto's in challenge. "You *said* you loved me—once."

"It was true—once."

DAPHNE CLAIR lives in Aotearoa—New Zealand, with her Dutch-born husband. Their five children have left home, but drift back at irregular intervals. At eight years old she embarked on her first novel, about taming a tiger. This epic never reached a publisher, but metamorphosed male tigers still prowl the pages of her romances. Her other writing includes nonfiction, poetry and short stories, and she has won literary prizes in New Zealand and America.

Books by Daphne Clair

Daphne *Clair*

EDGE OF DECEPTION

Harlequin Books

TORONTO • NEW YORK • LONDON
AMSTERDAM • PARIS • SYDNEY • HAMBURG
STOCKHOLM • ATHENS • TOKYO • MILAN
MADRID • WARSAW • BUDAPEST • AUCKLAND

ISBN 0-373-11749-3

EDGE OF DECEPTION

Copyright © 1995 by Daphne Clair de Jong.

First North American Publication 1995.

CHAPTER ONE

HE HADN'T CHANGED.

It was Tara's first thought when she saw him across the big, crowded room. There must have been nearly forty people there, standing about in groups with glasses in their hands, some of the men as tall as he, but her eyes found Sholto unerringly, as though he'd called her name. As though her heart, her mind, her body, had recognised his presence and known where to look for him.

What had brought him back to New Zealand?

Business, of course. Herne Holdings, his import and export business, still had a branch in Auckland as well as others in Hong Kong and Sydney, shipping goods from country to country all around the Pacific rim.

Perhaps it was the intensity of her gaze that made him turn his head from the woman at his side and meet Tara's eyes. She saw the small movement, quickly controlled, that betrayed his discomposure. Something flared in the Prussian-blue eyes below the dark slash of his brows, something compounded of recognition and antagonism, sending a hot shiver along her spine. And then he shifted slightly so that a broad shoulder in expensive charcoal tailoring partially obscured his companion, his sleek black head bent to concentrate on what she was saying.

'What can I get you to drink?' Chantelle was asking at Tara's side. 'Dry white? Or sparkling?' Her brown eyes, peeking from under a bouncy fringe, were enquiring.

'I'd like a stiff gin and lemon,' Tara heard herself say, wrenching her attention away to focus on her hostess. 'Happy birthday,' she added. 'As instructed, I didn't bring a present, but I'd love you to pick something you'd like from my shop. Pop in any time.'

She scarcely heard Chantelle's delighted rejoinder.

Maybe she should just leave. But that would entail some kind of explanation—and besides, Sholto had seen her. She didn't want him to think she was running away.

She avoided looking in his direction as she accompanied Chantelle to the polished mahogany bar in the corner of the room—which was two rooms, really, the dividing doors pushed back for the party.

Chantelle's husband, Philip, appeared and greeted Tara with a kiss on her cheek. 'What can I get you?' he asked, slipping behind the bar.

Chantelle relayed Tara's request.

'Hard day?' he enquired. The doorbell pealed, and Chantelle hurried off to answer it. Philip poured a generous measure of gin into a glass and topped it with lemon squash, adding a couple of ice cubes and a slice of fresh lemon before handing her the glass. 'Business booming in the antique trade?'

Tara took a swallow of the drink before answering. 'Real antiques are rather slow to move, but I'm doing well with other things. Furniture recycled from used native timber taken from demolition sites is a good seller. The prices are not as high as for antiques, so more people can afford them.'

'Swings and roundabouts, eh? Chantelle says she's selling more potted plants than cut flowers these days. Sign of the times, do you think?'

A man plonked a couple of glasses down on the curved bar, gave Tara a friendly, interested smile and said, 'Same again, please, Phil.'

Tara returned the smile briefly and took a couple of steps away, burying her nose in her glass. Philip had made the drink strong; maybe it would calm her leaping nerves.

'Tara.'

She knew he was near just before the deep, midnight voice spoke behind her. A spot between her shoulder blades, bared by the off-the-shoulder flame-red party frock and the swept-up style she'd imposed on her unruly burnished-bronze hair, felt as though a fiery finger had touched it.

Unconsciously standing taller, she turned slowly, making sure her face revealed none of her feelings, praying that her eyes, more green than hazel when her emotions were disturbed, would not betray her.

'Sholto.' She moved her lips in what she hoped was a reasonable facsimile of a smile. 'I didn't expect to see you here.'

'Nor I you.' Close up he was as devastating as ever, but her first impression had been wrong. There were subtle changes—a fine crease between the black eyebrows, a few more at the corners of the fathomless smalt eyes, and his mouth looked harder, without the faint promise of tenderness that had once been implicit in its firm lines. The light gleamed on his hair, and she realised with a pang that a few strands here and there had turned grey.

'You look older,' she said involuntarily. He would be thirty-eight now.

Not even trying to smile, he said, 'I am—five years older. So are you—but you don't show it.'

'You needn't flatter me,' she said with a hint of tartness.

'I wasn't.' His gaze moved over her in a chillingly clinical way. 'You've changed, but not aged. Hard to believe that you're—what?—twenty-seven.'

'Thank you.' Tara's voice was curt. She took another sip of her drink. 'Are you in Auckland on business?'

He seemed to hesitate before saying, 'Not entirely, this time.'

Someone bumped into her back, propelling her forward a little, the liquid in her glass slopping up to the rim but not spilling. Sholto reached out and closed his warm hand about her arm, steadying her.

'Sorry!' A man holding two beer glasses aloft stepped into her vision, a flustered smile on his face.

'It's all right,' she murmured.

Sholto still held her; she could feel his fingers on her flesh like a brand. He turned, bringing her to his side. 'We can't stand about here,' he said. 'I'll find a quiet corner where we can talk.' He began steering a path through the crowd, taking her with him.

Tara resisted. 'We should have talked a long time ago, Sholto. It's a bit late now.'

His fingers tightened fractionally, impatience in his face as he angled his head towards her. 'I've got something to tell you.'

What could he possibly have to say to her? 'Tell me here.'

A man on the outskirts of a laughing group must have heard the combative note in her voice. He looked round curiously, momentarily catching her eye.

Sholto's breath feathered her ear as he bent to speak into it. 'Believe me, this isn't where you want to hear it.'

He didn't relinquish his grip, and reluctantly she went with him. Better to capitulate than make a scene.

He led her through a doorway into a short passage and, opening another door opposite, found a switch and turned on the light.

'Philip's study?' Tara hesitated. Chantelle's husband was the advertising manager of a community newspaper and brought some of his work home. The small room was dominated by a wide desk on which stood a computer surrounded by paper trays and folders. Shelves and filing cabinets lined the walls up to the ceiling.

'I'm sure Phil won't mind.' Sholto drew her inside and shut the door before releasing her arm. There was very little space to move, even though Sholto remained standing just in front of the door.

'Sit down,' he said.

The only chair was a leather-covered swivel one before the desk. Tara glanced at it and said, 'No, thanks.'

She felt at enough of a disadvantage without having him tower over her. As long as she remained standing in her high-heeled red shoes there was only a matter of inches between their respective heights.

Sholto looked at her thoughtfully, then shrugged.

'So, what's the big secret?' Tara asked.

'It's no secret—that's rather the point.'

'If it isn't a secret, why on earth did you need to drag me in here? It's going to look a bit rude, you know. I've barely arrived.'

'I know exactly when you arrived.' His teeth snapped together.

Fleetingly Tara wondered if he'd been as aware of her presence as she had been of his, even before he looked up and saw her.

He said, 'I wish I'd known you were going to be here—'

'If I'd known *you* were going to be here I'd never have come!'

'Do you hate me so much, Tara?' he enquired softly.

Dark lashes swept down to conceal the look in her eyes. 'As much as you hate me.'

The silence stretched. Then the beautiful, spine-tingling voice spoke at last. 'I never said I hated you.'

She looked up, her eyes holding his in challenge. 'You *said* you loved me—once.'

'It was true—once.'

She had thought she'd got over being hurt by him, buried her feelings for him in the grave of their dead love. But the dispassionate admission somehow found an unguarded place in her heart, making her inwardly wince.

'No,' she said, striving to equal his coolness. 'You lusted for me. I don't believe you know what love is.' Maybe he was incapable of either love or hate. Of any really strong emotion.

He didn't move, and his face remained stony. 'If that's what you want to believe,' he said, as though it didn't matter to him.

She had never *wanted* to believe it. She'd come to that conclusion inevitably, as the result of bitter heartache. His indifference still stung. But she'd matured since their last encounter. 'Why don't you spit out what you want to say,' she invited him, 'and let me go back to the party? I came here to enjoy myself. And I'm sure the lady you just left is missing you.'

'Still a good-time girl?' he jeered, his hands going into his pockets as he leaned back on the door. 'All right. This isn't the time and place I'd have chosen, but I'd rather you heard it from me than as party gossip. I would have written to you, if I could find your address. I'm getting married. The *lady* I left just now is my fiancée.'

Thank God for make-up. Would the light foundation, the touch of blusher, hide the sudden drain of colour from her cheeks? She fervently hoped so. Her hand made a small movement, an involuntary groping for the chair, but she quickly halted it. She wasn't going to let him know that she felt as if she'd been punched in the midriff, that a strange, hollow void had just opened somewhere near her heart.

Despite the casual stance, his eyes were watchful, as though he was getting ready to catch her.

I won't let him have the satisfaction, Tara vowed. She lifted the forgotten glass in her hand and swallowed most of the drink, giving herself time to recover. Her voice was admirably steady when she said, 'Congratulations. You must introduce me. She does know about me?'

'Of course.'

'Well—' she gave him a bright, unseeing smile '—I hope it works out for you both.'

'Thank you.' His voice was clipped, and for the first time she thought she discerned a faint discomfort. 'You're here alone, tonight?'

A pity she hadn't arrived with some gorgeous man in tow. Trying to recall the woman Sholto had been with, she had a vague impression of pale, smooth hair falling to white, sloping shoulders, of a full mouth and compact curves. 'Yes, I am,' she admitted, 'this time.'

'I'm surprised.'

'From choice,' she assured him coolly. Not that it was any of his business.

A tight smile touched his mouth. 'I never imagined otherwise. Trawling, are you? I don't suppose you'll leave on your own. You're as lovely as ever—to look at.'

Her eyelids flickered at the brief, deliberate pause. She hoped he didn't realise how deep the barb had gone. 'Isn't it time we went back?'

'Yes.' Decisively he took his hands from his pockets and opened the door, waiting for her to precede him.

A perverse impulse stopped her as she was passing him, her eyes defiantly lifting to his. 'I wish you luck,' she said, and leaned forward to place a light kiss on his mouth.

That was what it was supposed to be—proof that she wasn't shattered, that she wished him well. But, tantalised by the warm familiarity of his mouth, the seductive scent of his skin, her lips lingered wistfully.

She felt an answering movement of his mouth, and his hands gripped her shoulders as his lips opened and drove against hers.

'Sholto?'

At the sound of the enquiring feminine voice, he thrust Tara away so roughly that her back came jarringly in contact with the door frame. She saw the fierce desire in his eyes before they turned murderous and then he dragged them from her to the woman standing hesitantly by the open door to the lounge, where the party went on noisily behind her.

'Averil.' Sholto held out his hand, stepping forward to draw her to his side.

As Tara shakily straightened herself, Sholto put his arm about the other woman. 'This is Tara,' he said, his voice hard, uninflected. 'I've told you about her. Tara, I want you to meet Averil Carolan, my fiancée.'

CHAPTER TWO

AVERIL GAVE HER a stiff smile. Her eyes were the light, almost achromatic hue of bleached denim. Although she wore high-heeled shoes, her head was barely level with Sholto's black tie, the pale hair contrasting with his jacket as his arm curled possessively about her shoulders. There'd be blond hairs adhering to the fine wool when he took his clothes off, Tara thought.

Banishing the picture edging into her mind, she held out her right hand. 'How nice to meet you. I was just giving Sholto my best wishes for you both.'

Averil's hand briefly met hers. 'Thank you.' She glanced up at Sholto, whose expression was enigmatic, his eyes resting on Tara with suspicion lurking in their depths.

The solid feel of the glass tumbler in her left hand was comforting. She tried a social answering smile, and asked, 'When is the happy day?'

'Soon,' Sholto said, as Averil answered, 'We haven't decided—' and then looked at him again, apologetically.

Sholto explained, 'There hasn't been time to discuss the details. We only bought the ring yesterday.'

So the engagement was new. 'I'm sure you'll work something out.' Tara kept the smile in place. Turning it on Averil, she said, 'May I see it—the ring?'

Averil's left hand was half concealed in the pastel pink folds of her skirt. Tara saw it clench before it was reluctantly proffered for her inspection.

The large oval diamond flanked by two smaller ones suited Averil's slim, tapered fingers and pink-painted nails.

'Lovely,' Tara said perfunctorily, her own ringless fingers clamping even harder on her glass. Tipping it to her lips, she emptied it completely. 'Well, I think I'll get myself another drink and join the party. Have a good time, you two.'

She turned away from them, making blindly for the lounge doorway and wending her way back to the bar. No one was there, but she helped herself to more gin from one of the variety of bottles standing on the counter, splashing a liberal amount into the glass before adding squash. Her hand shook and she spilled a few drops.

When she looked about, the room seemed to blur before her eyes, the sounds of chatter and laughter rising to a raucous hum until she wanted to cover her ears.

She held herself tightly together, taking three deep breaths. Perhaps she shouldn't have poured another gin. The final humiliation would be to get herself drunk and do something stupid. She'd snatched a couple of sandwiches at lunchtime, between customers, and had eaten nothing since. Although she'd never felt less hungry, some food would be a good idea.

As she went in search of it, a warm male hand fell on her shoulder. 'Tara! Chantelle said you were here! I've been looking for you.'

'Andy—' Tara turned with resignation. Andrew Paget towered over her, a wide grin showing perfect teeth that went with his over-long flaxen curls, guileless summer-sky gaze and carefully nurtured, brawny frame. A dazzling white T-shirt two sizes too small accentuated his sun-bed tan, and designer-label dress jeans lovingly hugged dramatically muscled thighs and calves.

She couldn't help smiling back at him. Andy had that effect on women. There was not a lot between his surgically flattened ears to complement the magnificent body and the Greek-god face, but she'd known him when he was an undersized kid with unevenly mown sandy hair and a mouth full of brand-new dental braces. Behind the fragile self-assurance engendered by a late growth spurt and the correcting of his disastrous teeth and ears, followed by a determined regimen of body-building, lurked the child who had endured the nickname of 'Wingnut' from the day he started school.

Tara had always had a soft spot for him during the two years they'd both attended the same school, before her father sold his hardware business in a Waikato town to invest in a new business selling how-to books to supermarkets and garages, then later bought out a surplus goods firm in Auckland. When Andy turned up years afterwards working in a sporting goods store in the small suburban mall where Chantelle and Tara had their own shops, his metamorphosis had stunned and amused her.

The women his new image attracted had improved Andy's confidence considerably, but that in no way changed the basic sweetness of his nature. Only, his conversational powers were extended by any discussion that ranged beyond football, pop songs, the innards of cars and the esoteric mysteries of body-building. He'd got his job less, she suspected, on any perceived sales ability than on the advertising value of his mere presence, kitted out from the store's range of expensive sports clothing.

'What did you want me for?' she asked him.

His grin widened. One thing Andy had learned from the parade of women competing for his delighted attention was a rather obvious form of sexual banter. His gaze dropped innocently over the figure-hugging red dress that stopped well short of Tara's knees and returned to her eyes, mischief dancing in his.

Before he could say anything, she told him crisply, 'I need to eat. Put those muscles of yours to good use, will you, and carve me a path to the food?' She'd glimpsed a couple of tables against the wall of the other room, laden with filled dishes.

Andy took her hand and did as she'd asked, fetching up before one of the tables with a look of triumph. Tempted to say, 'Good boy,' and pat him, she settled for, 'Thank you.' As she picked up a plate and began placing a selection of nibbles on it, she added, choosing her words more carefully this time, 'Why were you looking for me?'

Shoving a sausage roll into his mouth, Andy apparently swallowed it whole. 'Chantelle said you're on your own.'

'Yes, I am.' She hadn't brought anyone because she figured that would make it easier to slip off home early. These days parties tended to pall after a couple of hours, and she usually avoided them. Did Chantelle think she'd be lost without a partner?

Looking round idly, her gaze skittered away from Sholto and Averil, talking to Philip and another man. Chantelle didn't *know*, did she? No, she told herself. If she had, she'd have warned me.

'So'm I.' An oyster patty followed the sausage roll, leaving a fragment of pastry on his lower lip.

'What?' Absently she reached up and removed the flaky crumb, dropping it onto the edge of her plate.

'Alone,' he explained. 'I don't know anyone.'

Light dawned. Andy was *shy*, and had made a beeline for the one person he knew well. Childhood insecurities died hard. 'I don't know many people, either. Shall we stick together?' She smiled at him kindly, then bit into an asparagus roll, cool and bland.

Andy picked up another from the table and popped it into his mouth. 'Chantelle introduced me to this woman,' he muttered, furtively looking about the room. 'Over there.' Quickly he averted his eyes, and Tara's curious glance over her shoulder failed to identify which woman he meant.

'Didn't you like her?' she asked, finishing the roll and picking up a club sandwich. Andy was almost fatally friendly. She couldn't imagine him taking an instant dislike to anyone, especially a woman. He was so over-whelmingly grateful for their interest that he practically fell over himself trying to please them.

'Like her?' He looked as though the concept was beyond him. 'She—she's a professor! At the *university.*' His expression was one of awe bordering on terror.

Tara bridled. What had the woman done—deliberately intimidated him? If so, she was both cruel and a snob. It wasn't Andy's fault that he'd not been blessed with an academic brain like some people. 'What did she say to you?'

'Say?' He looked at her blankly. 'Not much. "Hello," and "What do you do?" is about all, really.' He swallowed. 'I g-got her a drink and then took off to find you.'

'What's wrong with her?'

'Nothing. She doesn't *look* like a professor. But how could I talk to her?'

'Just the same way you talk to me.' If the professor didn't like football, cars or pop music, she could at least have pretended to. Maybe she'd learn something. But maybe Andy hadn't given her the chance.

He shook his head. 'She's one of those *intelligent* women. What could I say to her?'

A smile lurking on her mouth, a pastry case filled with creamed corn poised in her hand, Tara raised her brows at him.

Andy looked at her silently, then blushed to the roots of his golden locks. 'Sorry, Tara! I didn't mean you aren't—I just meant—I mean, *she*—'

Tara laughed aloud, placing a comforting hand on his bronzed arm and patting it. 'Never mind, I know what you meant. I was teasing you.'

Relief washed over his superb features. 'Oh—good. That's all right, then. I wouldn't want to offend you, Tara.'

'You haven't.' She picked up her drink and hooked a casual hand into his arm. 'Come on, let's circulate.'

She didn't particularly want to circulate, but she wasn't intending to lurk in corners all night, either. Unable to stop her eyes from travelling to where she'd last seen Sholto, she found her gaze colliding with his dark stare. His eyes flicked to Andy and back to her face, a corner of his mouth momentarily curling in contempt before he looked away.

Shaken and hot with rage, she tightened her grip on Andy's substantial arm.

'Ow!' he protested, looking down at her in surprise.

Hastily she loosened her fingers, horrified to see the curved indentations of her fingernails showing red against his hair-dusted tan. '*Andy!* I'm sorry!'

Recovering, he grinned. 'Just give me warning next time, huh? Women don't usually mark me there! If you like I'll show you—'

'No, I don't like,' she said repressively. 'Behave yourself or I'll throw you to your professor and leave.'

'*Awp!*' He looked cowed. 'I'll behave, promise!'

Tara put on a friendly smile and without difficulty struck up several conversations, watching Andy regain some assurance as the women predictably reacted to his looks and diffident charm, and the men regarded him with covert envy.

He seemed to be getting on with a group of mainly young people who shared his musical taste, and she was murmuring an excuse to leave his side when he grabbed at her hand and said in lowered but panic-stricken tones, 'Don't go away!'

A young woman with a cuddly figure and halo of short, gingery corkscrew curls had joined the group, and one of the others said, 'Jane—have you met Tara and Andy?'

'Hi, Tara.' Jane gave Tara a smile that lit her rounded, unpainted face, and then turned to her companion. 'Andy and I met earlier, didn't we?'

Andy nodded, a strangled sound rising from his throat. His fingers convulsed around Tara's, making her suck in her breath, but she heroically refrained from complaint.

This was Andy's professor?

'I couldn't help overhearing what you just said about the ThreadBears,' Jane told him. 'Hardly anyone's heard of them yet, but in my opinion they're the best group this country's produced since Crowded House.'

'You *like* them?' Andy sounded stunned.

'I think their music is really interesting,' Jane said. 'Don't you? Did you see their latest video clip on TV last night?'

'You *like* the ThreadBears?' Andy repeated.

'Yes, I do.' Jane's smile faded as she looked enquiringly up into his face, and then widened again. 'I know,' she said resignedly. 'You thought I'd only be interested in fossils or dead languages or logarithms or something.'

Cautiously, he said, 'What are logarithms?'

'I've no idea,' Jane answered cheerfully. 'I've always been too intimidated to ask. Something to do with maths. My field is popular culture.'

Perhaps she wasn't quite so young as her curls and fresh complexion made her appear.

It took a few minutes for Andy to progress from uneasy monosyllables to entire sentences, but Jane's enthusiasm and her respect for his opinions soon opened him up. He gradually relaxed his death grip on Tara's hand, eventually freeing it so that he could wave his own hand to make a point.

'I'll fetch some more drinks,' she murmured, taking his empty beer glass in nearly numbed fingers. He hardly noticed as she slipped away.

Near the bar a few people were dancing to a tape player. One of the guests was dispensing drinks, and Philip was among the dancers, his arms wrapped about his wife.

'Been married fifteen years, those two,' the man behind the bar confided as he poured a beer for Andy and an iced tonic for Tara, 'and look at them. Beauty, isn't it?'

Tara smiled, hiding a pang of envy. 'Yes,' she agreed. 'They're very lucky.'

She picked up the glasses and turned carefully, to find her way blocked by a white designer shirt and charcoal dinner jacket. Sholto, holding two empty wine glasses.

He was inches away, both of them halting suddenly to avoid a collision. He looked at the drinks in her hands and said softly, so that only she could hear, 'Doesn't Lover-boy have the manners to fetch his own drink—and yours?'

'He's having an interesting conversation. I offered.'

'Conversation?' Sholto drawled. 'I have it on good authority that the guy's as thick as a couple of four-by-twos and his conversation is on a level with Neanderthal man's.'

Tara might have admitted the general premise, but she'd never have put it so brutally, nor discounted Andy's many and not unimportant virtues. Angry, she said, 'Jealousy will get you nowhere, Sholto.'

'Jealousy? Over *you?*' The contempt was back, in his voice. 'Dream on, darling.'

Annoyingly, she flushed. As he made to walk round her, she said, 'I wasn't talking about me. Almost every man here is jealous of Andy's physique—and his looks. Just as every woman admires them.'

'*Every* woman?' His brows rose.

'Is Averil an exception? Well...' she paused pointedly, then shrugged '...perhaps,' she conceded doubtfully. 'There's no accounting for taste, is there?'

'Perhaps she's not as easily impressed by the flagrantly obvious as...some.' Sholto turned his head, his eyes going towards the group about Andy's large frame. 'Hadn't you better get back to him, though? He probably has a short memory span.'

Involuntarily her eyes had followed the track of his. Jane, her lively, piquant face uplifted, was talking animatedly, while Andy grinned down at her, fascinated. 'There's nothing wrong with Andy's memory,' she said. 'Does Averil know about yours?' If he was going to hit below the belt, he could expect to be hit back.

'Mine?' His eyes narrowed, gleaming under the thick lashes.

'Does she know you're likely to forget that you're married?'

'I never *forgot* that I was married,' Sholto said bitingly after a loaded moment. 'There was no chance of that.'

'You could have fooled me,' she said, giddy with the knowledge that she'd made some impression on his apparent imperviousness. 'You did fool me for a while.'

'You fooled yourself.' His voice hardened, dark satin over steel. 'It was you who wrecked our relationship, Tara. You believed what you wanted to, and indulged in a childish revenge. Well, it doesn't matter to me now.'

She couldn't answer that—he always managed somehow to have the last word.

He stepped around her and went up to the bar, and she returned to Andy's side and stayed there for the rest of the interminable evening, leaning on his shoulder and pretending to listen, and laughing at the appropriate times.

When the crowd began to thin out and a surreptitious survey showed no sign of Sholto and his fiancée, she found Chantelle and said good night. 'Lovely party,' she added.

'We enjoyed it,' Chantelle said. 'Are you all right?' Her eyes turned searching, shrewd.

'A bit tired, maybe.'

'Philip said you were talking to Averil's fiancé.'

'Sholto—yes,' Tara said steadily. 'Do you know him well?'

'Averil's Philip's cousin, though they don't get together very often, she's away so much. Is Sholto a friend of yours?'

Tara shook her head. 'Not exactly. I hadn't seen him in years. Well, thanks again.' She turned away, making for the door.

Outside the house, the quiet suburban street was lined with parked cars. She walked rapidly along the pavement towards hers, looking round as she heard footsteps behind her.

'It's only me,' Andy said.

'I didn't realise you were leaving, too.' She waited for him to fall into step beside her. 'Did you bring a car?'

'Yeah, but I'll pick it up in the morning. I've had a couple too many beers.'

'How are you getting home?'

'Walk it off, I guess. Maybe I'll pick up a cruising taxi later.' They passed under the shadow of an overhanging tree, and Andy stumbled, flinging a heavy arm over Tara's shoulders to help regain his balance. Automatically she hitched her own arm about his waist, shoring him up. 'Thanks,' he said. 'Never could hold my liquor.'

'Why drink it, then?' Tara asked reasonably. She hadn't noticed him drinking all that much.

'Aw, come on,' Andy protested. 'A man's gotta—you know.'

'Not necessarily.'

'I was okay until the fresh air hit me.'

He still had his arm about her when she stopped by her car. 'You'd better get in,' she said. 'I'll take you home.'

'You don't hav'ta do that.'

'You're not safe to walk in your condition.' She lifted his arm with two hands and slipped out of his hold to go round the car and unlock the doors. The latches leaped up with a loud *thung*.

Andy rested his arms on the roof of the car as he smiled muzzily at her. 'No one's going to mess with me,' he assured her.

He was probably right. But there were other dangers for a man in his state. 'You could get hit by a car,' she argued.

He put his chin on his linked hands. 'I'm not that drunk, honest.'

Tara opened her door and stood holding it as she looked over at him. 'The door's unlocked. Get in.'

'Nah.' Andy shook his head. 'I'm okay.'

'You are not okay! I'll take you home.'

He straightened finally. 'All right, then. Thanks.' He opened the door and folded himself into the seat.

With a sigh of relief, Tara slid into the driver's seat beside him. 'Do up your safety belt.'

'Wha'?' He was leaning back, eyes closed, his hands loosely dropped between his knees.

'Your safety belt.' She sighed and reached across his substantial bulk to pull it down from its housing and across his broad chest to the clip between the seats. 'There.' She fastened her own belt and started the car.

Andy snoozed all the way, and she wondered if she'd have to help him inside, but the nap seemed to help sober him, and when she dropped him outside his flat he thanked her nicely and walked slowly but almost steadily to his door, waving at her before he closed it behind him.

'That's my good deed for the week,' Tara muttered to herself as she drove away. At least it had diverted her for a while from thinking about Sholto. And his impending marriage.

Black depression hit her, and she swallowed hard. Damn him, why did she have to meet him again? Just when she was able to spend days at a time, even whole weeks, without thinking of him?

TARA SLEPT BADLY in spite of the late hour that she'd gone to bed. Dressing in the morning for work, she chose a summery, low-necked frock printed with yellow daisies in the hope that it would cheer her up and detract attention from the hollows under her eyes. Thank heaven it was Saturday and at lunchtime she could shut up the shop and spend the rest of the day alone. Last night she'd had a surfeit of people.

She and her assistant, Tod Weller, were kept busy all morning, leaving her scant time to stand about thinking. She stayed after Tod had gone home, nibbling on a filled bread roll from a nearby cafe while she rearranged the stock, not because it needed it really, but to give herself something to do.

She hauled a couple of recycled-wood chests from the rear of the shop to the window, and draped two bright linen tablecloths across their corners, allowing much of the fabric to fall on the floor. Then she placed some smaller things among the folds—a glass paperweight, a bronze statuette, a branched candlestick of gleaming brass.

Her stock was an eclectic range of old and new. She specially loved antiques and second-hand knick-knacks, but also appreciated the brash colours and exciting forms of modern design, and the exotic charm of craft objects from other countries. Tara's special talent, she'd been told, was her ability to juxtapose styles in unexpected combinations that enhanced the qualities of each. She stocked anything that took her fancy and that might catch a customer's eye.

She spent the remainder of the afternoon pottering, and it was almost five o'clock when she opened the door and stood in the doorway fumbling in her bag for her key.

She had the key in her hand when she became aware of someone behind her and looked around, startled.

He was a big man, wearing a dark-visored motorcycle helmet that obscured his face. Steadying her breath, Tara said, 'Can I help you?'

His voice was muffled by the helmet. 'Money.'

Tara's heart lurched. She tried to step back and slam the door in his face, but he was too quick for her, pushing it hard so that it swung back and she had to move further inside to avoid being hurt.

And, of course, he came after her. 'Money,' he repeated. 'What do you do with it?'

'I . . . it's gone,' she lied. There was a small safe in the back room where they kept the takings and the cash float over the weekend, but it was well hidden behind an oriental hanging on the wall. 'I don't keep money in the shop.'

He gave her a shove and grabbed at the bag in her hand, upending it so that everything fell on the floor, including her wallet. Snatching that up, he opened it, pulled out the several notes that it contained and stuffed them into a pocket of his leather jacket before throwing the wallet on the floor again. 'You've got a safe,' he said. 'Show me!'

He was probably guessing. But even if he was he might be prepared to use violence before he'd be convinced. Better to lose her takings than risk that.

She thought about it a bit too long, saw his hand make a fist and tried to dodge, but he caught her cheek and sent her staggering against a solid oak sideboard, painfully banging her head, hip and elbow on the wood, and sending a small china jug to the floor, where it smashed to pieces.

Her instinct was to retaliate, but there was no weapon within reach and common sense dictated compliance. Besides, she was a little dizzy from the pain of the blow to her head. 'All right,' she said hurriedly, 'I'll show you.'

She took him into the back room used as office and storage space and pulled aside the hanging, opened the safe without a word and handed him the tin cash box.

The man stowed it bulkily inside his jacket and pushed her again. 'What's in there?' he demanded, nodding his helmeted head towards the door behind her.

'It's a toilet.'

He grabbed her arm and shoved her inside the tiny room. 'Stay there,' he ordered. 'Don't come out for twenty minutes or you'll be sorry.' He slammed the door.

Tara leaned an ear against the panel, closing her eyes in a mixture of relief and hope. She heard his booted feet on the floor, and the muffled voice shouted, 'Twenty minutes! Or you'll get it.'

He was making his getaway, not hanging about to see if she obeyed. She knew that, but her ears strained, her heart thudding. Had he gone all the way to the door? Would he wait for a minute—five, ten? Or just run? Was that the roar of a motorbike she could distantly hear? What direction did it come from?

She was shaking. The painted wood against her ear, her cheek, felt cold. She wanted to be sick. How long had she been standing here, too afraid to get out, to move?

The longer she delayed the more time he had to get away. Cautiously she turned the door handle, then paused. Nothing happened. She opened the door a crack, holding her breath, peering through the inadequate aperture. Still nothing.

Gathering her courage, she opened the door properly, looked through the connecting doorway to the shop. The place seemed empty. The telephone was on the desk in one corner of the back room. She dived for it, and with trembling fingers dialled the emergency number.

HOURS LATER she opened the door of the turn-of-the-century Epsom cottage she'd restored and refurbished, and thankfully closed it behind her. The police had been great, but trying to remember every detail that would help them and poring through photographs of likely suspects had taken its toll. Someone had given her coffee and a biscuit, and the phone number of a victim support group.

Her legs were unsteady as she walked across the dimmed living room, drawn by the light blinking on the answering machine sitting on a graceful antique writing bureau. She turned on a side lamp and pressed the play button on the machine, listened to a message from the library about a book she'd requested, another from a friend offering to sell her a ticket to a charity concert, and then jerked to attention as Sholto's voice filled the room. 'I'll phone again later,' he said, adding, 'It's Sholto,' as though she didn't know his voice, didn't react to it with every pore.

He had phoned again later, and again, each time with the same message, leaving no number for her to return the call.

Tempted to replay the tape just to hear his voice again, Tara clenched her teeth and reset it instead. She wasn't a mooning adolescent now; she was a grown woman and she'd got over Sholto. Not easily, but at last. There was no way she was going to fall into that maelstrom of emotion and pain again. If he did repeat his call she would let the machine deal with it.

In the kitchen she opened the refrigerator and her stomach turned at the sight of food. Closing the door, she made herself more coffee and nibbled on a dry cracker. And found herself back in the living room, leaning against the door jamb and staring at the phone.

When it rang she almost dropped the half-finished coffee in her haste to intercept the rings before the machine cut in. Snatching up the receiver, she managed a breathless, 'Hello? This is—'

'Tara,' Sholto said. 'I've been phoning you all day.'

'I was at the shop,' she said. 'I heard your message—messages.'

'You work in a shop?'

He didn't know, of course. 'I *own* a shop. Bygones and Bibelots. Mostly it's just called Bygones, though.'

'Antiques?'

'Yes, and some new stuff. A mixture.'

'You work late.'

'No, not really.' She swallowed, remembering the man in the dark-visored helmet. The shadows in the unlit corners of the room were deepening and she had a sudden urgent desire to turn on all the lights in the house. 'What did you want?'

'I shouldn't have said some of the things I did last night.'

Tara didn't answer immediately. Was this some kind of apology? Although his tone was aloof rather than conciliatory.

'I was caught off balance,' he said.

'So was I,' Tara admitted. She'd said some fairly waspish things herself. 'I wasn't expecting you there.'

'I suppose I spoiled the party for you.'

It *was* an apology—or at least probably as near as Sholto was likely to come to one.

'Th-that's all right.' Dismayingly, she heard her voice wobble. Tears slid hotly down her cheeks. 'It was j-just unlucky, I guess.'

'Tara?' His voice sharpened. 'Are you all right?'

She *wasn't* crying because he was marrying someone else, she told herself fiercely. It was too humiliating that he should think so. 'Yes,' she whispered.

'Tara—what is it?' He sounded cautious.

She could put the phone down. Only he'd be sure then that she was crying over him. 'Nothing,' she said. 'I got robbed, that's all—'

'*Robbed?*' For a moment there was silence, before he said urgently, 'Where? At your shop? Are you hurt?'

'N-no,' she gulped. 'Not really—not badly.'

'Do you have someone there with you?'

'No.'

'I'm on my way.'

'Sholto—no! I'm all right.'

But he'd already hung up and all she heard was the hum of the dial tone.

CHAPTER THREE

THE DOORBELL buzzed imperatively fifteen minutes later.
Tara had spent the time stemming the stupid tears, rins-
ing her face in cold water and rather unsuccessfully trying to cover up the aftermath of her crying jag with
make-up.

She didn't switch on the passage light and avoided
raising her eyes to Sholto's as she opened the door and
said quickly, 'You had no need to come rushing over.
How did you know where to find me, anyway?'

'Your address is in the phone book.' He stepped inside and closed the door himself, and then his hard
fingers lifted her chin, and he reached out his other hand
to the light switch by the door.

His brows contracted as he saw the swelling on her
cheekbone. He cursed under his breath. 'Have you seen
a doctor?'

'The police surgeon checked me over. It's only bruises.'

'*Only!* There are others?'

'A couple. You know I bruise easily. I was lucky—it
could have been worse.' She shivered, thinking how much
worse it could have been, and folded her arms across
herself, turning away. 'Now that you're here, you'd better come in.' She led the way to the living room.

'Your back!' he exclaimed, and as she looked round,
startled, he said, 'The bruise on your back, it's already
gone blue.'

Tara flushed. She'd forgotten about it, although she'd
had to invent a story for the doctor. She'd noticed a bit
of stiffness after she got up this morning, but there was

nothing visible when she peered in the mirror, and she'd thought no more about it as she donned the dress that dipped even lower at the back than in front. Over the afternoon the bruise had evidently coloured up, although it couldn't have been too bad earlier. Tod hadn't noticed. 'That must have happened last night,' she said.

'Last night?' he repeated sharply. 'What did that great ape do to you?'

Tara gaped at him. 'If you mean Andy—'

'I mean the guy you were draping yourself over all night, the one you brought home with you, even though it was obvious he was smashed out of his mind.'

'He was not! And what makes you think I brought him home?'

'I saw him get into your car. As a matter of fact, I thought you were trying to argue him out of it—I was half out of *my* car, intending to come to the rescue, when you leaned over and kissed him, so I figured you didn't need help after all.'

Kissed him? She'd leaned over to fasten Andy's safety belt. She supposed that from a distance it might have looked like an embrace. 'Where were you, anyway?' She'd thought that he and Averil had been long gone by then.

'Sitting in my car, some way behind you.'

So what he'd seen could only have been through the windows of other parked cars. And he'd jumped to conclusions.

But surely they'd left the party before she had. Why hadn't they driven off? Necking, she supposed, not able to wait until they got to—where? Averil's place? Or did they share? 'Couldn't keep your hands off each other?' she heard herself suggest. 'How sweet! Just like a couple of teenagers!'

Something flickered in his eyes. His mouth straightened. 'Actually, we were blocked by another car. The party appeared to be breaking up, so we thought we'd wait a while until someone moved it.' Not that it was any of her business, his tone implied.

Neither was her taking Andy home any of his. But she said, 'I drove Andy to his flat—and left him there.'

'Too far gone to perform, was he?' Without waiting for her comeback on that, he said, 'So where did that bruise come from?'

Tara let her lip curl derisively. 'Don't you remember?'

His brows drew together. 'Remember what?'

'When your fiancée found us kissing last night—'

'*You* kissed *me!*' he interrupted harshly.

There was no reason, Tara decided, to let him get away with that. She tipped her head to one side and smiled, slowly. 'When you were finishing what I'd started,' she said deliberately, 'and we were interrupted, you shoved me against the door frame—rather hard.'

He'd already been turning to Averil then, and by the time he'd looked back at Tara she'd been standing upright again.

Colour darkened his cheekbones and quickly receded, leaving them oddly sallow. '*I* did that?' he queried finally.

Tara nodded.

He hauled a rasping breath into his lungs. 'I had no idea!' He sounded almost shaken.

'It wasn't intentional,' she conceded. 'I do realise that.' 'Does it hurt?'

Tara shook her head. 'I'm not permanently damaged—by either you or the robber.'

She thought he almost winced. 'Where did it happen?' he asked. 'The robbery—at the shop?'

'Yes. He made me open the safe and took all this morning's takings.'

'Is that much?'

'Quite a lot. It was a busy morning. I'm not thrilled about it, but it won't put me out of business.'

Sholto moved further into the now well-lighted room, looked quickly at the two roomy, comfortable sofas, the faded oriental rug, the old heavily framed pictures, the antique bureau in one corner, the exotic wall hangings, and then returned his gaze to Tara's face. 'You were upset when I phoned.'

'Reaction. You were the first person, apart from the police and the doctor, that I'd spoken to since it happened.'

'How are you feeling now?'

'I'll be all right. It was kind of you to enquire, but unnecessary.'

He glanced again about the room. 'You live alone?'

'Yes. What about you? I mean,' she added hastily, 'where did you come from, tonight?' Was Averil waiting impatiently somewhere for him? She couldn't quite bring herself to ask.

'I'm staying in a hotel in the city. Averil's parents live in a small flat.'

And was she staying with them, or with him at the hotel? 'Chantelle said Averil's away a lot. What does she do?'

'She's a flight attendant.'

'The Hong Kong route? Is that how you met?'

'Yes. Aren't you going to ask me to sit down?'

She hadn't expected him to stay. Tara shrugged. 'Do you need an invitation? Please sit down, if you want to.'

'And you?' He indicated politely.

She sank onto the nearest sofa, and he sat on the other one, at right angles to hers, his arm resting on the back as he twisted to face her.

'So...how have you been?' he asked her.

The deep, quiet voice sounded caring, sincere. She thought she'd probably fallen in love with Sholto's voice before she'd fallen for the man. Marginally. Her almost instant emotional involvement had been cataclysmic— she'd scarcely had time to draw breath before she was in over her head.

And floundered for nearly three years, until the next cataclysm had propelled her out of his life, leaving her alone and struggling to stay alive.

Not in material terms, of course. He'd made sure she was financially amply provided for—conscience money, she had told herself bitterly. But emotionally she'd been annihilated, and it had taken her years just to regain some kind of equilibrium.

Last evening she'd discovered how fragile that equilibrium was. The news of Sholto's engagement had sent her spinning. All night she'd been reliving in her mind every detail of their ultimately disastrous relationship, besieged by grief and despair. She wondered if Sholto had ever experienced even a twinge of regret.

'I've been fine,' she told him. 'I have a very nice life.'

It was true, if one went by the surface things. She had a small but adequate circle of friends, a thriving if modest business, a delightful little home in a fashionable and pleasant suburb. Epsom was an area of desirable real estate, well-established and only minutes from the centre of Auckland city, but tranquil and almost crime-free, with tree-lined streets and a high proportion of gracious older homes among newer, architect-designed dwellings.

She didn't have a lover. Didn't want one, she reminded herself firmly. She preferred her life as it was—conventional and uncomplicated.

'And you,' she said, 'are obviously thriving.' He looked more confident, more handsome than ever. And he'd just got engaged to a woman who was pretty and presentable in every way, even if, in Tara's possibly biased opinion, a trifle colourless. 'I suppose business is booming?'

A small shrug. 'It's doing well,' Sholto conceded. He looked down at his polished shoes for an instant, and then up, with an air of deliberation. 'I'm going to be running it from Auckland again. Averil wants to settle here. She comes from a close-knit family.'

'Is she giving up her work?'

'Giving up flying, anyway.'

'Had enough of the high life?' Mentally Tara slapped herself. Bad puns weren't any way to conduct a sophisticated conversation.

Sholto's eyes sharpened for a second. 'She wants children.'

Did he know how much that hurt? Probably not, but he'd been defending Averil, all the same. Driven by some obscure demon, Tara said flippantly, 'And you'll be happy to keep her barefoot and pregnant, I suppose.'

He moved abruptly, dropping his arm from the sofa back and linking his fingers on one long, impeccably trousered thigh. 'I'll be happy to keep her happy,' he said softly.

She'd asked for that. With an effort she refrained from closing her eyes, staring unblinkingly into his until hers stung.

'Well,' she said then, 'you've assured yourself I'm still in one piece, and I expect Averil will be waiting for you. Thanks for your concern—' She stood up rather quickly and then gasped as the room spun before her surprised eyes. 'Oh!'

A hand gripped her arm. 'Sit down,' Sholto ordered, and pushed her back onto the sofa. 'Are you sure that doctor examined you properly?'

'Yes. I'm not concussed or anything. Just a bit of delayed shock, I expect. I shouldn't have got up so fast.' Experimentally, she moved her feet, ready to try again.

Sholto bent and scooped them onto the sofa. 'Don't move! When did you last eat?'

'Um—I had a cracker when I came home, with coffee.'

'A cracker!' he said with disgust.

'I wasn't hungry. At lunchtime I ate a filled roll.'

'One roll?'

'It was quite substantial,' she protested.

'Do you have any brandy?'

'You know I hate it.'

'I'll make you some more coffee. Where's the kitchen?'

'You can't—'

'*Where's the kitchen?* Never mind, I'll find it.'

'I'm really all right, now—'

He was already walking out of the room. At the door he looked back at her and said, 'Stay there.'

Tara subsided. Humiliatingly, she felt tears gathering again. It was such a long time since anyone had looked after her, and tonight she was feeling vulnerable. The afternoon's experience had affected her more than she'd realised.

When Sholto returned with a steaming cup she took it from him gratefully. He sat down on the end of the sofa by her feet and said, 'You've got no food here.'

'I was going to get a few things on my way home,' she said, 'but everything else that happened sort of killed that idea. There is bread, and a couple of eggs. And I'm sure I've got packets of pasta meals in the cupboard.'

Sholto grimaced disparagingly. 'Drink that up,' he said, 'and I'll take you out for supper.'

Tara nearly spilled the coffee she was sipping. 'You can't! What about Averil?'

'Averil is somewhere in the skies over Asia at this moment,' he drawled, glancing at his watch.

'Even so, what will she think about you spending the evening with me while her back is turned?'

'I said supper,' he reminded her mildly. 'Nothing more. And Averil isn't the jealous type.'

Tara lowered her eyes and took some more coffee. Averil, it seemed, was a paragon of all the virtues. 'Will you tell her?' she asked, realising that she'd tacitly agreed to go out with him.

'Probably,' he replied indifferently. 'I certainly won't be making a secret of it.'

And would Averil be as complacent about it as he obviously expected? Tara wondered. She hoped he wasn't in for a nasty surprise.

When she'd finished the coffee he said, 'Do you want to change?'

With a visible bruise on her back she'd better, Tara supposed. As he stood up, she gingerly brought her feet to the floor.

'Take it slowly,' Sholto advised, grasping her arm. 'Do you need any help?'

'No, I'll be okay.'

'Take your time,' he reiterated, 'there's no hurry. Yell if you need me.'

She walked to the bedroom as he watched her, and firmly closed the door.

With a bit more care and attention this time, she managed to almost disguise the mark on her cheek, and the sea-green cotton dress she put on had sleeves and zipped up to her neck at the back, although the front was moderately low. She fastened her hair up with several pins and a Victorian tortoiseshell comb.

When she came out of the bedroom holding a small bronze leather bag, Sholto was lounging in the living room doorway, his arms folded, looking patient. He looked up and she saw a stirring in his eyes that took her back eight years, to when they'd first known each other. She paused, and he straightened, his hands falling to his sides. 'Very nice,' he said, his voice clipped.

He turned away to open the door for her, and they stepped outside.

His car, a sleek, roomy, dark blue vehicle, was parked on the road outside. He ushered her in and she subsided onto the smooth leather.

'It smells new,' she said as he got in beside her.

'It is.'

Of course, she thought wryly.

'I took the liberty of using your phone while you were in the bedroom,' he told her. 'As it's Saturday night, I've booked a table.'

'Did you have trouble?'

'I tried a couple of places. This one is in Mount Eden. Okay?'

Mount Eden Road curved its way about the base of the dormant volcano and stretched along several miles to meet up with Mount Albert Road at a busy intersection. There were a number of good restaurants along its meandering length. 'That's fine,' she said.

The restaurant was full, but not very large, and the service friendly and efficient. Perusing the menu, Tara began to feel hungry. 'Pork with apricot sauce,' she decided, and when Sholto suggested a bread basket selection to start with, she agreed.

'Tell me about your shop,' he invited as she nibbled on a piece of crusty herbed bread.

Her tension eased as she described how she'd been working in an antique shop for a time, and later bought one that sold mainly second-hand junk, gradually getting rid of the stock until she'd achieved a more upmarket image.

'And that's been successful.'

'Very.'

He said thoughtfully, 'I'd never pictured you as a businesswoman.'

'I had some expert help from several people.'

'Anyone I know?' His eyes rested enigmatically on her while he absently tore apart a slice of olive bread.

Tara stiffened. She tried to sound casual. 'Derek Shearer gave me some advice.'

Sholto's strong fingers flicked some crumbs to the side of his plate. 'Derek's a first-class accountant.'

He wasn't looking at her. Tara forced herself to relax. 'Yes, he still does my tax return for me every year.'

The deep blue gaze pinned her suddenly. 'I'm sure that's not all he does.'

'He's a good friend. As you should know.'

'Really? Perhaps that's a matter of opinion.'

The air between them was charged, now. Tara's hand convulsed on the napkin in her lap, crushing the starched linen. Her mouth was dry.

'Who else...helped you?' Sholto asked. He leaned back, making an effort, she thought, to appear nonchalant.

Tara swallowed. 'Lots of people,' she said vaguely. 'You wouldn't know them. The other shopkeepers have been good to me. It's a small centre, and we all help each other when we can.'

Sholto nodded, and picked up his knife to spread a butter curl on his bread.

Over their main course he asked, 'Where do you get your stock from?'

'Various places. The antiques and collectables from second-hand dealers, opportunity shops, auctions, flea markets, the new things direct from craftspeople—woodworkers, potters, embroiderers. I even sell a few books—nicely bound old volumes and limited editions printed on a hand-operated press by a local couple. And quite a lot of imported goods from Asia and the Pacific Islands.'

'I could help you there.'

'I don't need your help!'

His brows lifted at her sharpness, and she said, 'Thank you.'

He gave a short, breathy laugh. 'Touchy, aren't you? Let me put it another way. Maybe we can do business together.'

'Why?'

'Why?' Sounding slightly impatient, he said, 'How do you think I built up *my* business? I make it a policy never to pass up an opportunity. You retail Asian and Pacific goods—I import them. We might both benefit from—using each other.'

'I thought,' she said delicately, 'we'd found that unsatisfactory.'

Sholto shoved his plate to one side, although there was still some food on it. Leaning forward, he said, 'I was talking of business—commerce—but if you insist on making this personal, just be sure you really want to cross swords with me.'

Tara's fingers gripped her fork hard. For a moment she kept her eyes fixed on the remains of her dinner, not sure why she had thrown that jibe at him. Sholto had never been one to ignore a challenge. Fatally, she could feel a stirring of excitement deep down. *Did* she want to cross swords with him? Was that what this edgy, half-pleasurable, half-painful tension that she'd felt ever since seeing him yesterday was all about?

Living with Sholto was a knife-edge experience, and one she'd vowed never to repeat. But in spite of the anger and hurt, and the bitterness that had accompanied the break-up of their relationship, she'd not felt wholly alive since—not until she'd kissed him last night in an act of reckless bravado, and been shaken to the core when he kissed her back.

'What can you offer me?' she asked obliquely.

She dared to look at him, and saw the narrowing of his eyes as he debated his answer. 'What do you want from me?' Before she had a chance to reply, he drew back in his chair, his expression changing to a smooth, urbane mask. 'I have silks from Japan, carved goods from Indonesia, woven hats and black pearls from the Cook Islands—'

'Pearls?'

'Pearls.'

'Aren't they very expensive?'

'Some are. The perfect specimens go to jewellers, mostly. But the odd-shaped ones that are not so valuable can make charming pendants, and some are still attached to the shell. A lot of people like those as ornaments.' He paused, regarding her thoughtful expression. 'Interested?'

'I'm always interested in unusual ornaments or jewellery. I don't go in for perfect strings of pearls or mass-produced stuff. But your odd-shaped black pearls—each one would be different, wouldn't it? That's what my customers like, something unique and quirky. I'd like to see some.'

'No problem. Tonight, if you like?'

'Tonight?'

'Why not? The warehouse is five minutes from here. I carry a key.'

They skipped dessert and had coffee and liqueurs. Both of them had drunk sparingly of the wine Sholto had ordered, and Tara had no worries about letting him drive her.

He turned towards the city, and eventually drew up in a car park outside a bulky, darkened building with a single light glowing outside. 'We'll go in the side door,' he said.

When they'd stepped inside he touched her arm in the darkness and said, 'Hold on, I'll deactivate the security alarm and get the lights on.'

He moved a few yards away, and then she blinked as fluorescent bulbs flickered and steadied and shed their pale light on tiers of shelving filled with boxes, piles of larger containers, and two forklift trucks parked neatly in a corner. 'There's a showroom upstairs,' Sholto said, and led her to an uncarpeted wooden stairway against one wall.

They climbed up into the shadows, and at the top Sholto paused to switch on more lights. A hand on her waist urged her forward, and she stepped onto a gleaming dark red rug with black and gold patterns.

It was like Aladdin's cave. There were more luxurious oriental rugs overlapping one another on the floor, shimmering silk wall hangings, a huge gold paper fan painted with peacocks and a black one with cherry blossoms. Appliquéd quilts in stunning colour combinations were heaped on a long trestle table, and carved coffee tables and sandalwood chests stood against the walls. Bamboo furniture held samples of teak carvings, and long strings of tiny stuffed animals with jewelled eyes and brocaded bodies hung from the rafters.

'The pearls are over here,' Sholto said, taking her arm in a light hold.

They were in a large display case. Sholto opened up the glass front and took out an oyster shell that fitted his palm. The moon glow of the mother-of-pearl gleamed in the fluorescent light, and embedded under its filmy surface were two luminescent black pearls, nestled side by side.

Tara touched them with a gentle finger, and Sholto said, 'Take it.'

She held the shell, warm from his hand, and said, 'This is lovely.'

Some of the shells in the case held one pearl, others two or even three. 'And here—' Sholto lifted out a tray covered in white satin '—are the pearls alone. These are all odd shapes.'

Several were quite large. She picked up one about the size of the bowl of a teaspoon that had formed into an almost perfect heart. 'This would sell.' It had the soft lustre typical of pearl, made mysterious by its black colour. 'How much?'

'Wholesale? We sell them in lots.' He turned aside and found a list taped to the side of the case, pulled it off and handed it to her. 'Here you are.'

She glanced down the price list. 'I'd like to order some.'

'Phone first thing on Monday and ask for Noel, the warehouse manager. I'll tell to him expect your call.'

'Thank you.' She relinquished the heart and said, 'I want that one in my selection.' She picked up another pearl, vaguely resembling a flower. 'And this.'

'Fine, just tell Noel.'

'One of my suppliers does jewellery at home. Maybe I could get her to set some of these to order for my customers.'

Tara replaced the flower and ran a fingertip over a cluster of fused pearls. 'They're nice to touch—that satiny patina over such hardness.'

He didn't answer, and she looked up enquiringly, to find him regarding her with an oddly brooding look in his eyes, his mouth curled faintly at one corner as if he'd remembered something unpalatable.

Tara dropped her hand and stepped back.

'Seen enough?' Sholto asked curtly.

'Yes. Of the pearls. Do you mind if I look around a bit?'

'Feel free.' He turned to replace the tray and close the cupboard.

She had caught sight of a number of huge floor cushions and beanbags crowded into a corner. She bent to pick up a cushion, and several more tumbled to the floor and lay on the rug around her feet. The cushion she held was covered in a patterned fabric of large birds and flowers, the design outlined with stitching and stuffed to give a raised effect.

'Like it?' Sholto had strolled silently over the rugs and was standing a few feet away, his hands in his pockets.

'Very much. Are there many in this style?'

He came over and helped her find some, each a different colour, a different pattern. 'Put the ones you want aside,' he suggested. 'I'll tell Noel to keep them for you.'

He helped her to pile them separately, and said, 'Is that the lot?'

'Yes, thanks.' She found herself too close to him as she straightened up, and stepped back hastily, catching her heel in the edge of one of the overlapping rugs and sprawling backwards as her shoe came off.

The rugs cushioned the fall, but surprise kept her from trying to rise for a moment or two.

When her eyes met Sholto's—a long way up—she blinked with shock. His mouth was clamped tight and his eyes were smouldering. *'Get up!'* he said harshly. And then, as though belatedly recalling his manners, he extended a hand to her.

Ignoring it, Tara struggled to her feet, only to falter on her unshod foot.

Sholto grabbed her arm. *'For God's sake!'* he muttered. She felt the brush of his breath against her cheek, smelled the scent of him—soap and wool suiting and an underlying masculine scent that evoked a rush of confused memories.

He swooped without releasing her and picked up her shoe, holding it ready for her. 'Here,' he said impatiently.

She looked down at his dark head and lifted her foot, felt him slide the shoe on. As she put her foot down again he straightened, his hold loosening. 'You didn't hurt yourself?'

Tara shook her head. 'Thank you.' The movement made her aware that a tendril of wavy hair had escaped down her neck. Sighing, she lifted her arms to push it back into place, taking out a pin to secure it. Which only made things worse, several more strands escaping to tumble over her neck and ears. 'Oh, damn!' she said as two gleaming pins fell to the rug. Her hair was the bane of her life. Thick and determined to curl, it was almost unmanageable when long, as now, but when she'd had it cut short she hated the way it went into childish curls all over her head, making her look like an elderly caricature of Shirley Temple.

Gathering the over-abundant mass in one hand, she bent to pick up the pins, then stood and ruthlessly twisted it into a knot, crossly relocating pins to keep it there.

Sholto had buried his hands back in his pockets. His voice sounding oddly strained, he said, 'You missed a bit.'

'Where?' She felt around and, discovering the ringlet just behind her ear, fumbled to tuck it in.

'Why do you bother?' Sholto asked. 'Most men would prefer it in its natural glory.'

He used to love her to wear her hair loose. He liked to play with it, arranging it about her head against the pillow, or pulling her on top of him and removing the pins so that her hair fell over her shoulders like a cloak, and then he'd tangle his fingers in it and draw her head down to kiss her while the bronze waves floated around them, cocooning them and drifting softly against his skin.

Tara jabbed a pin against her scalp, banishing the erotic picture from her mind. 'I'm not interested in pleasing *most men*,' she said. She just liked to keep her wild mane of elflocks under control and out of her way, and had never ceased wishing for fine, straight hair—like Averil's.

'Just one?' Sholto asked.

She looked at him and surprised a brief expression of chagrin on his face, as though he hadn't meant to say what he had.

She could have said, *Not even one*. But he had Averil, and her pride wouldn't let her admit to having no man in her life. She smiled enigmatically and said, 'Some men like it pinned up—they get a kick out of taking it down.'

His answering smile was thin and unpleasant. 'And I suppose you get a kick out of having them do it—among other things.' The way his gaze dropped over her body was enough to make her shiver. She'd never before met quite that blend of total dislike and blatant, deliberately offensive desire, stripping her defences as though he'd mentally undressed her.

Lust, she reminded herself, despising the way her senses burned in unspoken answer. If it had been anyone else but Sholto she would have been repelled by that look.

'You said you don't hate me,' she whispered, shaken.

'Hate you?' His eyes were veiled now, meeting hers. Mockery twisted his mouth. 'How could anyone—any *man*—hate something as decorative as you? I'd have to be a Philistine.'

'I'm not a *thing*.' She didn't know anyone else who had his ability to turn a compliment into a deadly insult. 'I'm a person, not some objet d'art.'

Not for the first time, she wondered if that was how he'd thought of her all those years ago—something pretty to enhance his home and his life.

'Your caveman loves you for your mind, does he?' Sholto rocked slightly on his heels, looking almost as though he was enjoying himself. Only the deep, angry spark at the back of his eyes gave him away.

About to shout at him, *Andy is not a caveman, and he's not mine!* Tara checked herself, forcing calmness into her voice. 'At least Andy recognises that I have one.'

Sholto's eyelids flickered. She saw the material of his trousers tauten across his abdomen as he clenched his knuckles inside his pockets. 'Meaning?' he enquired tersely.

'Meaning it's more than *you* ever did! Do you patronise Averil the way you did me? Is it her brains or her body that attracted you? Or couldn't you resist the idea of having your very own air hostess? I believe that's a common male fantasy.'

His face had changed subtly at the mention of Averil's name, almost as though she'd doused him in cold water. Was it possible that for a few minutes he'd forgotten about his fiancée?

'What would you know about male fantasies?' he jeered, but then he moved abruptly, taking his hands from his pockets. 'Come on, it's time I took you home. This conversation is getting out of hand.'

She couldn't agree more, Tara thought, relief and reluctance warring inside her as she walked beside him to the stairs. It hadn't been a comfortable conversation, but she'd felt the adrenaline singing in her veins. In an odd way she'd almost enjoyed skirmishing with Sholto, giving as good as she'd got. At least for a few minutes she'd felt truly, tinglingly alive.

CHAPTER FOUR

HE TOOK HER HOME and saw her to the front porch, standing by as she fumbled for her key.

'Thank you for the dinner,' she said, pushing open the door. 'And for... worrying about me.'

'My pleasure,' he said, 'if a little mixed.'

Tara gave a soft laugh. 'That goes for us both.'

'I suppose so. Will you be all right now?'

'Yes. I've hardly thought about the robbery all evening.'

'Good.' He hesitated a moment longer, and she wondered if he expected to be asked inside, but when she looked at him his eyes were focused on her mouth.

Tara blinked, her heart giving a hard thud against her ribs.

Then he was looking over her shoulder at the wall, saying in a strangely distant voice, 'I'm glad to have taken your mind off it. Have a good night's sleep.'

He turned and headed down the path.

ON SUNDAY he phoned. 'Just to check that you're okay,' he said, still with that detached note in his voice. 'No after-effects?'

'None,' Tara assured him crisply. The bruise on her cheek was coming out, going blue, but she wasn't a shivering jelly of nerves. 'I'm back to normal.' Almost. Her main emotion in regard to the robbery was anger; she wasn't going to allow a thug like that to have any long-term effect on her.

'I'm glad to hear that,' Sholto said formally.

'Thanks for enquiring.'

'Not at all.' He sounded positively cool now. 'Look after yourself.'

He had put down the phone before she could say any more.

SHOLTO must have been as good as his word. When Tara phoned the Herne Holdings warehouse on Monday morning and asked for Noel, she got a friendly greeting from a man who said he'd been expecting her call, and who failed to keep the curiosity out of his voice. 'Sure,' he said, when she asked for delivery of the goods she'd chosen. 'No problem. They'll be there this afternoon.'

When they arrived she arranged the cushions haphazardly in a corner, and placed some of the pearl shells with their trapped half-formed pearls on the two chests she'd moved into the window on Saturday. The single pearls went under the glass counter inside the door—it didn't do to keep small, valuable trinkets where light fingers could easily transfer them to pocket or bag.

'Nice,' Tod commented, picking up one of the shells. 'Where did you find them?'

'Herne Holdings,' she said briefly.

Tod, a rangy twenty-year-old whose olive skin proclaimed his part-Maori heritage and contrasted strikingly with light green eyes, pushed a long, glossy black curl off his forehead. She knew he thought it looked sexy, but he was forever shoving it away, torn between vanity and convenience. 'They're big importers, aren't they?'

'And exporters, yes.'

'Didn't know we dealt with them.'

'We do now. At least we have, this once.'

Tod adjusted the brocade waistcoat he'd rescued from a box of assorted clothing and linen Tara had got for a song at auction, and checked that the rolled-up sleeves of his white silk shirt were at the right length for a look of casual elegance. 'Thought they only supplied department stores and big furniture shops.'

Tara looked up from checking through her invoice book. 'They seemed quite happy to supply me.'

Two customers wandered in, and Tod turned his attention to them. 'Hi! Anything I can help you with?...Sure, you look around all you want, just give us a shout if you need information or anything, okay?'

He was a good salesman, not too pushy. She was lucky to have him, Tara thought. Sometimes a customer—usually an older woman—would string him along, asking questions, pretending to be interested in some purchase but unable to make up her mind, just to keep him dancing attendance because he was young and friendly and good-looking. When they left the shop he'd smile ruefully at Tara, and sometimes she'd tease him a little. Neither of them minded, really. There were a lot of lonely people in the world, and maybe another day the customer would come back and buy something.

Tod had been horrified at the news of the robbery, and bravely said that he wished he'd been there instead of Tara. 'I'd have seen him off,' he muttered darkly. 'He wouldn't have got *me* to open the safe.'

Tara tried to look impressed, biting her tongue. Mildly, she said, 'If you are here and it happens again, I don't want any heroics, Tod. Your life is more important than any amount of money. And that's the boss talking, okay?'

'Yeah, okay,' he reluctantly agreed.

If nothing else, she thought, he could save face by referring to boss's orders. Not, she hoped, that the situation would ever arise.

One of the pearls on a shell went that day, and two more on the next. 'We should order some more,' Tod said.

She'd contacted the woman who picked up shells, stones and bits of coloured glass washed up on beaches, combining them with gold or silver wire or chains to turn them into intriguing earrings, necklaces and bracelets. The craftswoman was thrilled at the idea of custom-made black pearl jewellery. 'I'd love to try it,' she said. 'I could never afford to pay for the pearls myself.'

Tara phoned Noel again and asked for another assortment of pearls in their shells to be dispatched to her shop.

'Sure thing,' he said. 'Anything else?'

'Well…' She was looking at a space on the wall left by the sale of a large rug that morning. 'You had some interesting South American rugs.'

'How many would you like?'

'Five. The small size.'

'Five it is. They're very popular. Sure you don't want more? A couple of the larger size, maybe?'

'It's not a big shop,' she explained. 'I don't have a lot of room to display them.' She'd been glad to see the other one go. It had been monopolising too much space for too long.

'Well, if you get rid of these, just phone for another lot.'

'I'll let you know,' she promised.

'Do that,' he urged. 'The boss said to keep you happy.'

Did he? Tara thought as she put down the receiver. You might have given some thought to keeping me happy all those years ago, Sholto.

The next morning a van with the Herne Holdings logo on it pulled into the service lane behind the shop, and two men unloaded several rolled rugs and a carton. One of the men was Sholto, dressed in jeans and a blue cotton shirt.

'Where do you want these?' he asked, standing with a couple of rugs slung over his shoulder.

Tara stared at him in surprise, then hurriedly collected her wits. 'Over there, please.' She pointed to a corner of the back room. 'Lean them against the wall.'

'Is this all the storage you have?' He looked around critically. The room was crammed with boxes and heaped with an assortment of stock that would be moved into the shop as space became available.

'I try to keep bulky things down here, rather than lug them up and down stairs. What are you doing here, Sholto?'

'Delivering goods,' he said, giving her a narrow, sardonic smile as the driver loped out to the truck again.

'You know what I mean!'

'Familiarising myself with the New Zealand operation again,' he said. 'And I was curious—'

The van driver walked in with some more rugs and stowed them with the others. He presented a delivery book to Tara and she signed it, taking the sheet that he tore out for her. 'Okay, boss?' he asked Sholto.

Sholto nodded, then looked at his watch. 'You have another delivery near here, don't you?'

'Yup. End of the street. Grumbley's.'

'I'll meet you there in fifteen minutes.'

When the driver had left, Tara said, 'Curious about what?'

'This place. Your shop. When Noel told me you'd put in another order I decided to come along for the ride. Want to show me around?'

It was early and they hadn't yet had a customer. Tod was arranging an assortment of colourful linen goods in a large, white-painted wheelbarrow just outside the front door when Tara led Sholto into the shop.

'Very nice,' Sholto said, taking a comprehensive look about. 'You've crammed a lot of stuff into a small space, but it doesn't look cluttered.'

'Thank you.' Tara was annoyed at herself for the pleasure she derived from his praise. She ought to have got over being dependent on Sholto for her self-esteem. She *had* got over it, she reminded herself. It was just that seeing him again had revived old emotions, old instincts.

Sholto examined an antique dresser and picked up a Victorian pipe rack, turning it in his hands before replacing it on the shelf. A half-round table with cabriole legs and curved drawers drew his eye for a few seconds, and he stopped before a handsome corner cabinet of mottled kauri, the shelves filled with flowered china and small figurines. 'Very handsome,' he said. 'How old is it?'

'It was made in Auckland in 1880. The cabinet-maker wrote his name and the date on the back.'

'Is it for sale?'

'If I get the right price.' She moved the card, which had somehow become hidden behind a bone china cup and saucer, placing it prominently on a shelf. 'I won't let it go for less.'

Sholto nodded, moving on. 'These are the chests you mentioned,' he asked, squatting down to see them better, 'made from recycled timber?'

'Yes.'

'You didn't tell me they were carved.' He ran his fingers, long and lightly tanned, over the simple but precisely executed design on the front of the chest.

'Some are. There's another in the window.'

'Hmm.' He walked over and touched that one too. 'This guy knows what he's doing.'

'Gal,' Tara said dryly. 'Woman, actually.'

He sent her a sharp glance. 'So, you've caught me out in a sexist assumption. Does she do the construction work as well or only the carving?'

'Both.'

He looked at the price ticket on the chest. 'I'd like to buy this one.'

Tara hesitated, curiously reluctant. She imagined him presenting the chest to Averil, the two of them deciding where to put it in their new home.

'Is there a problem?' Sholto asked, his brows rising.

'No, of course not,' she answered briskly. 'Will you want it delivered?' Presumably he wasn't going to try lugging the chest along the street. 'Are you still in a hotel?'

'No, not now. We'll pick it up with the van when we've finished the delivery run.'

Tod came inside, making the row of Chinese brass bells hung on the door tinkle as he opened it invitingly for the customers, and looked enquiringly at the stranger.

Tara introduced him. 'And this is Sholto Herne,' she told him, 'of Herne Holdings.'

'Yeah?' Impressed, Tod took Sholto's proffered hand. 'Pleased to meet you, Mr Herne.'

Sholto didn't return Tod's ingenuously friendly smile. His mouth looked stern, and he was regarding the young man rather searchingly. 'Were you about when this robbery took place?' he asked.

'No, sir. If I had been—I told Tara I'd have seen the bloke off.'

'Would you?' Sholto enquired dryly. His eyes ran over Tod's slight, youthful frame in a way that made the boy fidget uncomfortably. Looking away dismissively, he swept the shop with a gaze like a laser beam and said, 'What kind of security do you have here?'

Tara said, 'It's adequate for most contingencies. And all the retailers in the mall chip in to pay for an after-hours patrol. It's possible to get too security conscious and scare away the customers.'

He might have been going to argue, but she changed the subject. 'Tod, Mr Herne wants to buy that chest over there. Can you move the things off the top of it and we'll take it out the back. How do you want to pay for it, Sholto?'

He took a credit card from his pocket and handed it to her. 'You'll take this?'

'Of course.' Tara went to the counter and found a transaction slip.

'There's no need to shift the chest,' he said. 'The driver can help me carry it when we come for it.'

She was inserting his card in the machine, and didn't look up. 'Thank you, but I'll have it out the back for you, ready to load.'

Sholto frowned. 'Who's going to move it? That kid?'

She handed him the credit slip. 'Both of us. With two, it's not a problem.'

Sholto frowned. 'I'll help your assistant shift it before I go.'

'Your driver will be waiting for you.'

'He can wait. I'm not going to let you—'

'Sholto! For heaven's sake, we've shifted dozens of them between us. I moved two on Saturday on my own! They're not that heavy, just too bulky for one person.'

'Then how did you—?'

'I used my brains,' Tara snapped, causing Tod to cast a curious glance across at her as he placed the brass candlestick on a shelf. Lowering her voice, she said, 'I put each chest on a mat and slid it into position. Now will you stop being so bloody-minded and leave me to run my business in my own way!'

His eyes were dark, his jaw stubborn. But after a moment he lifted his hands and said, 'Fine. I'll pick up the chest later.'

By the time he'd signed the credit slip and taken back his card there was a customer browsing along the shelves of pottery and second-hand knick-knacks. Tod moved to offer assistance, and Sholto said quietly to Tara, 'Your young man is very decorative, but how much use is he likely to be?'

'Tod's extremely useful. He's a natural salesman.'

Sholto cast an impatient glance in his direction. 'Perhaps, but even if he'd been here on Saturday, could he have protected you?'

'I didn't hire him for *protection!*'

'All right, *helped* you, then,' Sholto amended. 'If you're going to have a man about the place, it might as well be one who can deal with a situation like that.'

'It isn't likely to happen again. And I'm not going to start choosing my staff on the basis of their muscle power!'

'Unlike your men friends?'

Her mouth tightened, and he said, 'Forget I said that. It's your life.'

'Yes.'

He jammed his wallet into the pocket of his jeans, nodded curtly to her and left.

When Tara heard the van arrive later in the service lane she let Tod go out and deal with the loading of the chest. She preferred not to face Sholto again.

AT THE END of the month the bill came from Herne Holdings. Sitting at her desk in the back room, Tara frowned at the account, surprised at the figure. Shaking her head, she reached for her calculator.

Five minutes later she was on the telephone to the warehouse manager.

'I think there's been a mistake,' she told Noel. 'Your account doesn't tally with the delivery notes I have.'

'No mistake,' he said.

Trying not to audibly sigh, Tara explained.

'Discount,' Noel suggested.

'There's no mention here of discount.'

'Must be an oversight, I guess.'

'It was a generous reduction. What's the percentage?'

Noel floundered. 'Um—ah, you'd have to ask the bookkeeper. Depends on the customer.'

Tara well knew that as Herne Holdings customers went, she was very small fry indeed. Suspiciously, she asked, 'Did the bookkeeper decide how much discount I was entitled to?'

'Um—not exactly.'

'And you didn't either.'

'Well, I—'

'Then who did?'

Silence for a few seconds. Then, cautiously, 'Look, you're not losing anything by it, Ms Greenstreet. What's your problem?'

Tara briefly chewed on her lip. It wasn't his fault, and she didn't want to make him uncomfortable. 'No prob-

lem,' she said brightly. 'Thanks for your help.' A brief
pause before she said, 'I don't have Mr Herne's phone
number. Could you give it to me?'

'Well,' Noel said, with obvious relief, 'he's got an office right in this building, now. Hold on.'

She didn't even have to go through a secretary. Sholto
was on the line in seconds.

'I've been talking to Noel,' Tara said crisply. 'I thought
there'd been a mistake in the account, but he says not.
Did you tell him to give me a discount?'

'Discounts are normal in business—'

'On wholesale prices? Not like this! I can't accept
favours, Sholto! Why did you do it?'

For a moment she thought he might not answer. Then
he said, 'I figured that after being robbed you could do
with a bit of a boost.'

'That was kind of you,' Tara said formally, 'but I don't
want special treatment. It was only one morning's
takings.'

'What is this?' he asked rather testily. 'Pride?'

'It's business! I won't have you—'

She was cut off by his laughter. 'In business any perks
are gratefully accepted. This is the first time I've heard a
customer complain about being *undercharged!*'

'If you gave all your customers this kind of con-
cession you'd soon be out of business, yourself.'

'I don't.'

'That's just the point!'

'A friendly gesture,' he said impatiently, 'to someone
who'd had a nasty experience, *business-wise*. I know you
shrugged it off, but for a small shop the loss of a day's
takings can be disastrous. You were telling me how the
other retailers had helped you out when you started. You
didn't throw *their* acts of kindness back in their faces.'

'Of course not, but this isn't the same—'

'Because it comes from me?'

'Because it's different!'

'How is it different?' Sholto challenged.

'Their help was...more personal. Advice and support, and an occasional helping hand. It didn't involve giving me money.'

'I haven't given you money.'

'You're splitting hairs.'

'I'm not in a position to give you personal help, as in physically being there—'

'I know,' Tara acknowledged hastily. Although on Saturday that was exactly what he had done. 'I don't expect anything from you, Sholto.'

'Take the discount, Tara, and stop fussing,' he said almost wearily. 'I promise that next time you'll be treated like any other customer, if that will make you happier.'

'Thank you,' Tara said stiffly. 'I appreciate that.'

'Anything to oblige a customer,' he said, not attempting to disguise the sarcasm in his voice.

TOD HAD TAKEN to hanging about until Tara locked up each evening. But one day just before closing time Andy wandered in, and Tod said, 'D'you mind if I go now, Tara? I've got a special date tonight. Andy'll be around for a while, won't you, Andy?'

'Sure,' Andy agreed. 'Go for it, Tod.'

'Yes, all right,' Tara said. 'See you tomorrow.'

When he'd left she turned to Andy. 'Did he ask you to keep an eye on me?'

'Um—not exactly. He just mentioned that he wanted to get away early, only he doesn't like leaving you on your own since the robbery. So I told him I'd make sure you weren't—on your own, I mean. The boss said I could come along before five.'

Touched, she said, 'That's awfully good of him—of all of you. But I really don't think it's necessary.'

Of course everyone in the mall knew about the robbery. Some had advised her to tighten security, get a grille on the window and install a better alarm system.

'I wanted to see you, anyway,' Andy told her. 'Want to ask you something.'

Tara went to turn the sign on the door to Closed. 'Yes?' she said. 'What?'

'D'you remember Jane? The . . . the—'

'The professor,' Tara supplied.

'Yeah. Her. Well . . . d'you think she liked me—really?'

'She certainly seemed to enjoy talking with you.'

Andy's face lit. 'I liked talking to her, a lot. I really had a good time that night. With you, too,' he added earnestly.

Tara laughed. 'Thanks. So, have you seen Jane again?'

'Not since then. Only, I've got this crazy idea.'

When he didn't elaborate, Tara gently prompted, 'What is it?'

'I thought . . . I thought I might ring her at the university, and . . . and ask her out. On a date. With me.'

'So?' Tara asked. 'What's crazy about that?'

Andy looked at her hopefully. 'You don't think she'd laugh at me?'

'Why on earth should she do that?'

'Aw, Tara, come on! She . . . she's an *intellectual!* I'm just a salesman. And you know it was all I could do to get a pass mark at school—in any subject!'

'I'm sure she isn't going to laugh at you,' Tara said firmly. 'She'll be thrilled and flattered—'

'Aw—' Andy shook his head.

'She will!' Tara insisted. 'Even if she turns you down, she's going to be delighted that you asked.'

'You do think she'll turn me down!' Andy said gloomily.

'I have no idea! But maybe she's in a relationship, or something. Do you know?'

'No. She wasn't with anyone at the party.'

'Ask her,' Tara said. 'She could be just waiting for you to call her.'

Andy snorted. 'She's probably forgotten all about me by now. She won't even remember who I am.'

Tara looked him over, from his glorious golden mane to his size-fourteen joggers. 'No chance,' she said. 'She's probably been dreaming about you every night.'

Andy blushed. 'Come on, Tara, be serious!'

'Don't tell me you don't know what effect you have on women,' Tara said sternly. 'You *work* on it!'

'Okay, so I do,' he admitted. 'And of course I like it when . . . when women come on to me. It's a buzz. But I don't really—I mean it's not serious stuff mostly, you know. Just kidding around. I don't . . . I mean, I'm not a stud. For one thing,' he said solemnly, 'it would interfere with my training schedule.'

Tara bit back a choke of laughter. 'That's good.'

'Jane's different. Those girls—well, I guess they like me because of . . . of how I look, you know?'

Tara nodded. 'And Jane liked you for your mind?'

Andy scowled. 'That's a joke, isn't it?'

She touched his arm. 'No, it's not. I didn't mean it to be. I'm sure she liked your personality, you have similar taste in music, and maybe how you look won't matter to her—but she can't have helped noticing, Andy. Any woman would!'

'It never made any difference to you.'

'I knew you when you were a grubby-kneed little brat. Jane didn't. Look, give her a call and see what she says. The worst that can happen is that she'll say no—for whatever reason. But you won't know if you don't ask her.'

'I'll take her to a film,' he decided. 'Then we won't have to talk much.'

'She *likes* talking to you.'

'D'you think so, really? We could have coffee afterwards. We could talk about the film, then.'

'Sounds good. What film are you thinking of?'

His brow knotted anxiously again. 'Maybe she'll want to see one of those arty things—with subtitles. Trouble is, I don't know anything about symbolism and stuff like that.'

'Ask her what she'd like to see,' Tara suggested. 'Her subject is popular culture. She might prefer a space opera or a Disney film.'

'D'you think so?' Andy began to look slightly happier. 'Okay, I'll ask her.'

JANE'S CHOICE was ultimately a fast-paced Hollywood thriller. Tara happened to be at the same theatre with Derek Shearer and they met Jane and Andy on the pavement outside afterwards.

Andy hailed Tara as though he hadn't seen her for a year, and enthusiastically invited her and Derek to join him and Jane for supper. 'We thought we'd go to Ponsonby,' he said. 'The cafes will still be open there.'

Along Ponsonby Road crammed and dusty second-hand shops and trendy boutiques rubbed shoulders in the daytime with greengroceries selling exotic fruits and vegetables from the Pacific Islands—coconuts and yams, taro and ugli fruit. At night the fruit shops and junk shops were shuttered, but the cafe society spilled onto the pavement out of the well-lighted interiors of establishments selling Turkish, Indian, Lebanese or Chinese delicacies or just an eclectic mixture of fashion foods.

The one they ended up at was relatively quiet. They found a table just inside the door, and ordered coffee and desserts.

Jane asked Derek what he did, and looked respectful when he explained he was an accountant. 'I'm hopeless with figures,' she confessed. 'I'd be useless in business. But I suppose you must be good at that sort of thing, Tara.'

Tara shook her head. 'Derek does my accounting.'

Derek said, 'Don't be so modest. You keep impeccable books. Balancing your yearly accounts is a breeze.'

'Heck, I can't even balance my chequebook,' Jane said.

'Can't you?' Andy looked at her in astonishment.

'Can you?' she asked him, laughing.

'Yes.'

Jane stared at him with exaggerated awe, until he blushed. 'Heavens!' she said. 'I don't know anyone else in the *world* who can do that!'

Looking at Andy, Tara saw him almost preen. Then he cast Jane a suspicious look. Finally he shrugged. 'Well, I can.'

The desserts came, and Derek asked, 'So what did you two make of the film?'

Tara thought Andy would wait to hear Jane's opinion before venturing one of his own, but he surprised her, launching into a fluent critique of the story, the acting and the photography.

Jane soon chipped in with her own thoughts, and Tara relaxed. Jane talked to him as an equal.

Pushing away her glass dish a few minutes later, Tara felt a slight prickle of awareness, almost apprehension, and lifted her eyes to scan the restaurant. Several tables away Sholto was sitting with a woman who had her back to Tara, but she recognised the pale hair and graceful sloping shoulders.

Sholto gave her a brief nod, and she returned a cool, minimal smile. She saw Averil lean forward to say something, and Sholto's lips move as he answered; his gaze leaving Tara.

Tara looked away. The others were laughing at some remark of Derek's, and she joined in without knowing what the joke was. She was out with friends, having a good time, and she didn't want anyone to think otherwise.

A little later Derek turned to murmur in Tara's ear, 'Sholto's here.'

'I know.'

'Are you all right?'

Tara gave him a smile. 'It's all water under the bridge, Derek. We've met a couple of times since he came back to New Zealand.'

'You have? And... how was it?'

Tara shrugged. 'No problem. The woman with him is his new fiancée,' she said, pleased that her voice hadn't faltered.

'Oh?' Derek's gaze travelled in their direction. 'Well, well.' After a moment he said, 'She doesn't look like Sholto's type.'

'I'm the one who wasn't his type, Derek. I was...an aberration.'

'Nonsense!' About to say more, Derek broke off and warned, 'They're coming this way.'

She was staring down into her empty sweet dish but she knew when Sholto stopped by the table, and reluctantly looked upwards.

Averil, pink-cheeked and pretty, had a hand tucked firmly into his arm. She was the first to speak. 'Hello, Tara,' she said.

'Averil. Nice to see you.' Tara shifted her eyes to Sholto's face and saw his mouth curve ironically. 'Hello, Sholto.'

'Good evening, Tara.' He flicked a glance at Jane and a slightly longer one at Andy, then transferred an inimical gaze to the other man at the table. 'Derek. Enjoying yourselves?'

'Very much,' Tara said crisply.

Averil said, 'I love this cafe. It's new since Sholto lived in Auckland last. I told him he *had* to bring me here!' She squeezed his arm with both hands and looked up at him adoringly.

Tara clamped her teeth together. Her gaze went glassy.

'Still the man about town, Derek?' Sholto said pleasantly.

Derek laughed. 'If you mean have I settled down, no,' he said, 'not yet. Although if Tara here would have me—'

Tara blinked, before she realised what he was doing. He thought she needed to save face, and was gallantly trying to help.

'Really?' Sholto drawled. 'I thought that you two had already—er—but never mind. Good night.'

'Good night,' Averil echoed brightly.

They left a silence behind them. Even Andy and Jane had caught the tension and were looking curiously at their companions.

'Damn him,' Derek muttered. 'He always was a sarcastic bastard.'

'Who is he?' Jane asked curiously. 'He was at Chantelle's party, wasn't he?'

He, Tara noted sourly. Averil had been with Sholto that night too, but it wasn't Averil that Jane remembered.

Derek spoke. 'He's Sholto Herne of Herne Holdings.'

'Um . . . I think I've heard the name, but . . .'

Tara said, 'He's my ex-husband.'

CHAPTER FIVE

'THAT'S your ex-husband?' Andy asked.

'Yes,' Tara answered shortly. 'He's been overseas for a few years.'

'Did Chantelle know you two when . . . ?'

'No. His fiancée is Philip's cousin.' She picked up her coffee and sipped at it, hoping the others would take a hint and drop the subject.

Jane filled the breach with a cheerful remark about her passionfruit sundae. 'Food straight from heaven,' she sighed, 'but I'll have to live on lettuce leaves for a week to make up for it.'

'Don't,' Andy said.

Jane shook her head firmly. 'With my figure—'

'There's nothing wrong with your figure.'

Jane laughed. 'That's sweet of you, but you don't have to lie—'

'I never lie,' Andy said simply. 'I just like you the way you are.'

Ruefully, Jane said, 'You're only—'

Tara confirmed, 'Andy's the most truthful person I know.'

'See?' Andy looked at Jane, giving her exactly the same deliberately sexy once-over that he'd turned on Tara at the party. Then he leaned towards her and murmured something in her ear.

Jane flushed speechlessly, and Andy sat back in his chair with a self-satisfied air.

Tara regarded him with mild anxiety. She wasn't sure how Jane would react to his turning on the charm. It was an act that went down well with some women, but was Jane one of them?

Certainly Jane was markedly quiet after that, but the flush hadn't entirely died from her cheeks, and her eyes had a soft glow.

A FEW DAYS later Chantelle came breezing into the shop. 'I've got twenty minutes to look for a wedding present,' she announced.

Tara's heart lurched. She swallowed. 'What...what sort of thing were you thinking of? Pottery, something to hang on the wall, or...'

'Not pottery. Table linen, perhaps. Nothing heavy. I have to post it to America, and I don't want the postage to equal the price of the gift.'

'America,' Tara repeated numbly.

'Something with a distinctly New Zealand look would be nice, but I don't want the souvenir type of thing. You know what I mean!'

Tara did know. Garishly painted native birds and flowers and crude pictures of early Maori life printed onto tea towels or tablecloths were all too common in shops catering to tourists. 'We have some hand-printed calico table mats with Auckland scenes on them. One Tree Hill, Waitemata Harbour, the view from the Waitakeres—that sort of thing. You can choose a set of identical mats, or different ones.' Tara led her friend to the old dresser with its invitingly opened drawers. 'Here they are. They're padded with nylon filling, and very lightweight.'

'Ideal!' Chantelle said with relief. 'I knew you wouldn't let me down.'

She made her choice and picked out a handpainted card to go with it.

'Do you want me to post them for you,' Tara asked as she giftwrapped the mats, 'or would you rather do it yourself?'

'I'll do it, thanks. I hope they like them. My niece is getting married over there, but I really don't know what her taste is.'

'There's nothing to dislike in them. The colours are muted, and the designs are lovely.' Casually, Tara added, 'Philip's cousin is getting married soon, too, isn't she?'

'Averil—yes.' Chantelle looked embarrassed, and lowered her voice. 'I didn't know about you and Sholto when I invited you to my party, Tara. I'd have warned you—'

Tara smiled. 'That's okay. We were both surprised, but it's no great tragedy.'

'Averil said you're still friends—you and him. It's always better to be civilised about these things, isn't it? Especially in a place like Auckland. I mean, you're bound to bump into each other.'

'Yes.' Who had told Averil they were friends? Sholto? 'There you are. I'm sure your niece will like them.'

'Thanks. You've been a great help.'

And you've been none at all, Tara thought, as Chantelle left.

Not that it made a whit of difference, really, whether Sholto and Averil had set a wedding date or not. She was rather glad that Chantelle hadn't recognised her polite query for the fishing expedition that it was.

ALL DAY Tara was unable to banish Sholto from her mind. The evenings were still long, and after having a meal she tied her hair back with a silk scarf and wandered about her small garden, pulling out a few weeds without enthusiasm. Bored and restless, she decided to go for a walk. Perhaps it would help her to sleep. Lately she had been lying awake for hours every night, trying to stop her mind from going back in time, replaying the years she'd spent with Sholto.

The suburban streets were quiet except for a few children romping on their lawns or riding bikes along the footpath, and an occasional dog warning her not to enter his property. Twice she met couples strolling arm in arm, and exchanged a smile and a greeting. And tried not to envy them.

She liked living in an old suburb. There was an air of permanence and solidity about the mature trees with thick trunks and spreading branches that spilled over garden fences and shaded the footpaths, and the solid, rambling weatherboard houses, some of them two-storeyed, built before Tara was born.

The air was fresh and clean, and the smell of new-mown grass mingled with the scents of magnolia, roses and jasmine. Tara's rubber-soled walking shoes made no sound on the still sun-warmed pavements.

When she turned back into her own street the light was becoming dusky, the sky above a washed-out pink. Her step faltered at the sight of a dark, raking car parked outside her gate. She told herself it wasn't, couldn't be, Sholto. But when the driver's door opened and he got out and slammed it behind him, she walked steadily towards him with a sense of fatalism.

He stood by the car watching her approach, and even at a distance there emanated from him a subtle air of tension. And when she reached her gate and put a hand on the worn curve of the wood, turning an enquiring look on him, he didn't move, just kept watching her with an unnerving, unreadable stare.

'You want to see me?' she asked. 'Have you been waiting long?'

'A while. Where were you?'

'Walking. It's a nice evening for it.'

'You go walking alone—at night?' He frowned.

'It isn't dark yet. Why are you here, Sholto?'

He dragged his gaze from her face and looked at her hand, still on the gate. 'Are you going to ask me in?'

Tara hesitated momentarily, then shrugged and pushed the gate wide. 'Come in and tell me what you want.'

She slipped off her shoes at the door, led him into the living room, switched on a lamp and indicated the sofa he'd sat on before. But he shook his head, standing instead with his hands in his pockets, a faint frown on his brow.

'Coffee?' she offered.

'No, thanks. But if you want one...'

'Not particularly.' She'd avoided coffee in the evenings lately, thinking that it would only exacerbate her problem with getting to sleep.

He prowled to the window, stood there briefly and then looked around the room as he had before. 'This room is...very unusual,' he said.

'Is that a polite way of saying it's an uncoordinated mess?'

'It's a way of saying I like it. Your taste in furnishings was always unexpected.'

'Unexpected?'

'It seems at odds with your personality.'

'Perhaps you don't know as much about my personality as you think.'

'After more than two years of marriage—'

'You hadn't begun to know me.'

He didn't answer directly, just looking keenly at her for a moment. 'Even then you wanted to fill our home with antiques.'

'Not *fill* it! Just have some about. I don't recall you objecting.'

'I didn't object at all. I'm not saying I didn't like your taste, just that I find it somewhat surprising.'

'Perhaps I have hidden depths.'

She spoke lightly, but his eyes were searching as they met hers. 'Perhaps,' he said noncommittally.

So he didn't think so. Tara tried to find some humour in that, and failed.

Sholto moved away from the window. Thinking he was about to take a seat, she sat down. But he'd stopped before one of the pictures, a panoramic landscape in a wide wooden frame. 'Is this a Hoyte?' he asked.

'I doubt it. It's unsigned, and I don't suppose it's worth anything, but I like it.'

'Where did you find it?'

'In a house lot from a deceased estate.'

'Ever had it valued?'

Tara shook her head. 'I wouldn't part with it anyway.'

He cast her an enigmatic look and turned to study another picture, then moved to the carved fire surround, and picked up a three-cornered green Wedgwood vase from the mantel, running a finger over the raised design on the china.

Unable to bear the silence any longer, Tara said, 'Is Averil working again? Where has she flown off to this time?'

Sholto replaced the vase and turned to face her. He leaned a shoulder with apparent nonchalance against the mantel, shoving one hand into his pocket. 'Bangkok.'

'She has an interesting life. And she's willing to give it all up for you?'

'I didn't ask her to give up her job. It was Averil's idea entirely.'

'Because she wants a family.'

'Yes.'

Carefully Tara drew in a quiet breath through her nose. 'I hope everything goes according to plan.'

Sholto's other hand went into his pocket, and he shifted his feet, crossing one over the other, looking down for a moment at the toe of his impeccably polished shoe. 'Do you, really?' he asked, his eyes suddenly meeting hers.

She looked back at him with a feeling of unease. 'I don't wish you ill, Sholto,' she said. 'I hope... you'll be very happy.'

'Do you think I will be?'

Taken aback, Tara replied, 'I... I don't think I'm the right person to ask.'

'I didn't seriously expect an answer.' He left the fireplace and went back to the window. 'Call it a rhetorical question.' He was standing side-on to her, looking through the glass with a remote expression.

'Sholto,' she said after a while, 'why are you here?'

'Impulse,' he said, facing her again.

Impulse? Sholto? Warily, she regarded him. Had he just been at a loose end because Averil was away?

He said abruptly, 'I think we have some unfinished business between us.'

Tara's heart seemed to leap into her throat. 'What...do you mean?'

He didn't speak for so long she thought he'd changed his mind. Finally he said, as though he was thinking every phrase through, 'I thought I'd put...our marriage behind me, that I was ready for a new relationship. Until that damned party. I found myself saying things I had no right to say—and feeling things I had no right to feel. I was unprepared—meeting without warning like that was like stepping into a time warp.'

It had been a bit like that for her, too. All the feelings that she'd suppressed so that she could go on living an outwardly normal life had rushed back to the surface.

'Then,' Sholto went on grimly, 'when I saw you at that cafe with two men dancing attendance—'

'Andy was with Jane,' Tara protested, 'not me!'

'Jane? Is that her name? It figures,' Sholto said cynically.

'What do you mean by that?' Tara queried sharply.

He gave her a withering look. 'You're not trying to tell me that your Incredible Hulk is really interested in *her!* What was it, a blind date you rigged up so you wouldn't have any real competition?'

Standing up to bring herself nearer to his level, Tara said, 'It was nothing of the sort. Andy doesn't need blind dates! He asked Jane to go out with him. And Derek and I just happened to meet them in town that night, so the four of us decided to have supper together. Actually Andy's very interested in her—not that I'm obliged to explain anything to you!'

'All right.' He took a couple of steps away from the window, running a hand over his hair and down the back of his neck. Looking at a point on the wall beyond her shoulder, he said, 'I have some unresolved feelings about—what happened to us. I don't want to carry that baggage into my new marriage. It wouldn't be fair to Averil. If you and I could...talk things out, it might help.'

'As I remember,' Tara said bitterly, 'you weren't that keen on talking things out five years ago.'

'There wasn't much point.'

'But there is now? You were the one who wanted a divorce,' she reminded him.

'Do you *know* what the alternative was?' he demanded.

'Alternative? What alternative?'

'I think I'd have killed you,' Sholto said flatly. 'And Derek.'

Tara's eyes widened, her lips parting. 'You're making that up,' she said. 'You were perfectly calm.'

His lips moved cynically in a semblance of a smile. 'Are you still as naïve as you were then?'

'I know you were angry—but it was such cold anger.' Without thinking, she brought her arms across her breasts to stop an involuntary shiver. 'There was no emotion in it.'

'You don't really believe that.'

'I mean there was no...no real passion.'

'*Passion?*'

'It wasn't personal,' Tara said stubbornly. 'I realise you were furious, but it had nothing to do with me as a person in my own right. It was because I was yours—your wife. And you thought Derek had...stolen something from you.'

There was a long silence. Sholto's brows were drawn heavily together as he stared at her, hard. 'Are you saying,' he asked her at last, 'that I looked on you as my *property?*'

Tara's arms dropped. 'Didn't you?'

'For God's sake, do you really think I'm that medieval?'

Tara shrugged. 'There are still men like that around. Plenty of them.'

'And I'm supposed to be one? Thanks.'

'It just seemed to have more to do with your pride, your self-image, than with us as a couple—our relationship.'

He shook his head as if to clear it. 'I don't *believe* this!'

'I'm just telling you how it looked from my perspective. I don't suppose for a minute that you saw it that way.'

'I never thought I owned you, Tara!'

'Never consciously, perhaps. And it wasn't entirely your fault. I was too young for marriage—I realise that, now. But I was dazzled by you.' She smiled wryly. 'Oh, I know you weren't in love with me—'

'Why do you say that?' he asked swiftly.

'I fooled myself at the time that you were,' she said, still smiling. 'Because I wanted it to be true—'

'Why,' he interrupted, 'do you think I married you?'

'Oh, several reasons. You were attracted to me on a physical level—'

'*Attracted* hardly covers it,' Sholto told her dryly.

'—after all, at nineteen, what did I have to offer a man of twenty-eight but a ripe young body?'

'There was no shortage of ripe young bodies I could have had for the asking—or at least, at a price. You've no need to put yourself down this way.'

Biting back her instinctive reply to his first statement, she said, 'I'm trying to be honest. That was one factor—and guilt was another.'

'Guilt?'

'As I told you at the time, you weren't to blame. I wanted you at least as much as you wanted me. And I knew even then that if you'd realised I was a virgin you wouldn't have made love to me. I know you felt guilty about it, and that was another reason you offered to marry me.'

'We'd been sleeping together for months before I suggested marriage.'

'On my twentieth birthday. Had you been waiting until you thought I was old enough?'

'If you must know, I was well aware that you were still too young. But I went ahead anyway because—'

Tara filled in the silence as he stopped in mid-sentence. 'Because you thought you owed it to me.'

'It was a lot more than that.'

'There were other reasons, of course. I'd been so dependent on you ever since my father's death, you felt responsible for me. But marriage—that really wasn't necessary, Sholto.'

'It was necessary for *me*,' he said harshly. 'Don't think I was sacrificing myself for you, Tara! Nothing could be further from the truth.'

'To square your conscience,' she said. 'I know. I think even at the time I knew, but I was very young, and I still had dreams.'

He was studying her with an expression almost of dislike. 'And just when did you work out this fascinating theory?'

She shrugged. 'Wisdom comes with maturity. I guess it's gradually dawned on me since our divorce.'

'You think I treated you like a sex object?'

'It was a bit more complicated than that.'

'At least you acknowledge that much!'

'I'm not holding you responsible, Sholto. You did what seemed right at the time. I'm sure you had the best of intentions.'

He raised his eyes. '*Sweet heaven!* Will you stop making excuses for me—do you think I didn't justify myself in my own mind a hundred times a day during our marriage? I was the adult, at the time. I should have known better!'

'That's the crux of it, isn't it?' Tara asked. 'You never did treat me as an equal. I was someone you felt responsible for, that you had to control just as you controlled your business and everything else in your life. Oh, you were right, in a way,' she added as he took a step towards her, scowling. 'I hadn't grown up. I should have confronted you on a rational, adult level instead of throwing tantrums and then making a stupid, juvenile attempt to get your attention. It backfired badly.'

'I'm sure there were faults on both sides,' he said formally, 'but you certainly found a way to get back at me for anything you imagined I might have done to you.'

'You still don't believe that nothing happened, do you?' Tara asked huskily.

'That's hardly the point.' She saw the tension in his body, heard it in his voice. 'If I'd arrived a few moments later—or earlier—I'd have found you in bed with my so-called best friend. Whether I discovered you before or after the fact isn't really relevant.'

'Sholto, I'm *sorry*—'

'That I do believe,' he drawled. 'You complain now, but at the time you enjoyed being married to me—at least in a material sense I was able to give you pretty much all you wanted.'

'Sholto—'

'Did you think I was so besotted I'd turn a blind eye—pretend I didn't care?'

'That was just what it was about!' Tara said desperately. 'That you *didn't* care! If you had you would at least have let me try to explain.'

'Explanations were a bit redundant, don't you think? How were you going to explain being in our bedroom with Derek, both of you half-undressed? It would have to be a bloody good story!'

'Sholto—believe me—'

'That's a great start!' He folded his arms, adopting an exaggerated attitude of patient listening, a faint sneer on his lips.

Tara stared at him helplessly, and swallowed. Then her chin came up and she resolutely met his eyes. Keeping her voice quiet and even, she said, 'You've already made up your mind not to listen, just as you did before. This isn't working, Sholto. I think you had better leave.'

He remained where he was, staring at her, and a new light came into his eyes, perhaps a hint of surprised respect. Finally he nodded and unfolded his arms. 'You're right,' he said. 'It was a bad idea.'

He walked past her with a bleak expression on his face. Tara followed him down the dim passageway to the front door, standing a foot or so behind him as he turned the knob to open it.

It was an old door and in humid or damp weather it sometimes stuck. When it didn't give immediately he tugged impatiently, and it came free so suddenly that his elbow jerked back, driving against her breast.

She gave a small cry of pain, a hand going to her breast, even as Sholto whirled with a muffled oath, and his fingers closed on her shoulders. 'Have I hurt you?'

'It's all right.' Instinctively she raised her face to look at him, and found him so overwhelmingly near that her voice faltered.

Even in the inadequate light she saw the gradual softening of his features, the dark fire in his eyes. His eyes were locked with hers and one of his hands moved slowly away from her shoulder and down, and as her own hand came to rest over her heart, his replaced it on her breast, warm and cherishing. 'Here?' he murmured, as his heavy-lidded gaze followed.

Her heart was thudding unevenly. She knew she should draw away, but was quite unable to. Closing her eyes, she whispered in agony that had nothing to do with the physical hurt, 'Sholto...'

His hand was stroking lightly, carefully, as though he was afraid of hurting her more. And his other hand no longer imprisoned her shoulder, but was at her waist, bringing her snugly to the hard warmth of his body. She flattened both palms against his chest, feeling the rise of his ribs through the thin cotton of his shirt. 'Sholto...'

'Why are you shivering?' His voice was deep and slow, as though he, too, was caught in a hypnotic spell, a magic web of sensation that bound them inextricably to each other.

'I'm...afraid.' She made herself open her eyes and look at him.

'Of me?' His hand stopped moving, but she was acutely conscious of it gently enfolding her breast.

'Of... of *this*,' she said tensely.

'*God!*' Sholto breathed roughly. 'You're not the only one.'

He bent his head almost unwillingly, and Tara's lips parted, trying to say, *No!*

But her voice refused to utter the word, and then it was too late. Sholto's mouth had found hers, and with a smothered cry she surrendered to his passionate assault on her senses. Her arms went up to his shoulders, then round his neck, while he kissed her as if only she could slake some long-starved, driving need within him.

His hand left her breast to rove over her waist and hip, then behind her, intimately shaping her lower body, splaying over the rounded curves and urging her closer so that she couldn't help recognising his instant arousal.

The scent of him was all around her, soap and fresh sweat and musk, and she felt him shudder as she moved longingly against him, spurred by memory and the erotic intimacy of the kiss.

He turned slightly, bringing her with him, wrapped his arms about her and eased his thigh between hers, sending a wave of heat throughout her entire being. One hand fumbled at her hair, drawing the confining scarf down its length, freeing the luxuriant waves.

Both hands in her hair, he withdrew his mouth at last from hers, and buried his face in the springing, soft abundance.

The darkness seemed to swirl about them. Tara's fingers were on the warm, damp skin of his neck, aware of the pulse beating unevenly below the surface. She tried to think, to fight free of the miasma of need and sensual enthralment that all but engulfed her; made a small, fluttery movement of negation, her breath brushing his cheek as she said, 'Sholto... Sholto! Why are you doing this? What do you want?'

She felt the sudden rigidity of his arms before he groaned deep in his throat and lifted his face, gazing down at her as though trying to make out just who she was.

Then he heaved air into his lungs and abruptly freed her, turning to smash both his fists against the wall, his forehead resting against it between them. The first, muffled expletive was something she didn't catch. He took another shuddering breath and said through gritted teeth, 'Damn you, Tara! You always were a witch. God, I should have known better than to come within a hundred yards of you!'

Silently Tara recoiled a couple of steps, her clenched hands pressed above her waist. 'I didn't ask you to kiss me,' she said raggedly. 'I didn't even want to see you!'

'I know.' He straightened up, but didn't turn to look at her. 'I know,' he repeated. 'It was my own stupid idea. I'm sorry if I've... raised any false expectations. We'll both get over it. Nothing a cold shower won't fix.'

He groped almost drunkenly to the door, wrenched it wider and slammed it behind him as he stepped into the night.

Tara's hands dropped to her sides, still clenched into fists. She wanted to throw something at the door—in lieu of Sholto's dark head. She'd like to smash something, knowing that he'd hear the sound of it, that he'd know her fury was directed at him.

She didn't need a cold shower. The finality of that slammed door was enough to quell the unbidden waves of desire that he'd evoked with such humiliating, devastating ease. She felt chilled now with reaction. Where the hell did he get off, barging into her home, her life, without an invitation, expecting her to help him sort out his problems with his prospective new wife, having the *gall* to start making love to her and then walk out like that? Let alone accusing her of bewitching him because he couldn't keep his raging hormones under control while his fiancée was away!

Well, she told herself cynically, locking up the house and preparing for bed, it was a novelty to be on the other side of the triangle—instead of the cheated wife she was the Other Woman, she supposed.

It gave her no satisfaction. It would have been expecting too much for her to actively like Averil, but she didn't hate her. Poor Averil—did she know what heartbreak she was letting herself in for, that Sholto couldn't be trusted out of her sight?

Perhaps she did. That could be why she'd decided to give up her flight attendant's job, because it would take her away from him too often. Staying home was probably a good move. And bringing Sholto back to New Zealand where, perhaps, temptation was less rife. Maybe she hoped that a family would tie him down.

'Good luck to her,' Tara muttered, as she bent over the basin to clean her teeth. Averil would be lucky if she managed to turn Sholto into a family man.

Tara still remembered his reaction when *she* had suggested they might start a family.

'Not yet,' he'd said decisively. 'In a few years, maybe.'

But in a pitifully few years their marriage had been over. Just as well they'd had no children to make the break even more traumatic. Firmly she pushed away the thought that if there had been children things might have been different. Surely Sholto wouldn't have been so ruthless if he'd had a family to think of?

Don't be such a fool, she scolded herself, her mouth tingling from the vigour of her toothbrushing. She rinsed it thoroughly and spat forcefully into the basin. He never thought of you as the mother of his children.

He'd made that very plain. He'd treated Tara herself almost like a child, except in bed. He'd never blinked at the bills for any purchases she made for their home, or the clothes she'd bought. But he had not talked to her about his work or shared his business worries, if he'd had any, had never asked for her opinion before making decisions.

The only reason he'd married her was his inconvenient conscience. And he'd leapt at the first real excuse she had given him to dump her without being totally in the wrong. He'd had to square that with his conscience, too.

Like most people, Sholto liked to look good in his own eyes.

CHAPTER SIX

TARA TRIED not to think about Sholto any more. She didn't expect to hear from him again, and told herself it was better that way.

But she was strangely restless, unsettled. She began seriously wondering what the future held for her.

Her business was established now, doing well in a small but comfortable way, and she had no desire to move into larger premises or open another shop. Empire building wasn't for her. That had been Sholto's specialty.

She had an adequate social life. Derek, who had never married, was always happy to escort her on the few social occasions when she needed a partner, and if he wasn't available some other male friend would oblige. She tended not to see them so often because experience had taught her that men sometimes wanted to advance the relationship beyond mere friendship.

Derek understood as no one else did. For some time she hadn't wanted to see him at all, but Derek had been worried about her, blaming himself. He'd probably saved her from a nervous breakdown, or worse. They had, not without difficulty and residual embarrassment, established a comfortable friendship, and she didn't want to change it.

She had persuaded herself that her life was all she wanted it to be. Now she was inexplicably wanting more, feeling a sense of urgency, of dissatisfaction, almost of panic.

Sholto was getting married again, taking a new wife and planning a family. Tara's personal life had been on hold ever since their divorce. She'd been jolted into an awareness of time ticking remorselessly on, of life passing her by.

Trying to shake it off, she accepted every invitation that came her way, determined not to sit about and brood on her fate. She should have realised, she told herself some time later, or perhaps she had subconsciously even hoped, that eventually she would accidentally bump into Sholto again.

It happened at a gala premiere evening for a New Zealand film. She'd agreed to attend with the set designer whom she had met a few times through mutual friends. He'd been scouting for historical artifacts for the film before it was shot, and had asked her to look for specific items that he wanted to incorporate into the sets. Tara had been able to provide a table lamp that delighted him, and several other small pieces, and she was intrigued to see them featured in the film.

Afterwards there was a party at a yacht club on the harbour's edge, attended by about two hundred people. Ruben, the set designer, introduced her to the stars of the film, the director, and several crew people, all thoroughly pleased with themselves and lapping up the compliments that came their way.

While someone wrung her companion's hand and congratulated him, Tara's wandering eyes caught a dark blue gaze, and her hand, holding a glass of white wine, trembled so that a couple of droplets spilled coldly onto her wrist.

Shamingly, she was immediately glad that she had bought a new dress for the occasion, a dramatic black and silver sheath with a low neckline that set off the striking pendant about her throat, a single fiery green opal set in silver.

She looked for Averil at Sholto's side, but although he stood taller than most of those around him, the crowd was such that she was unable to tell if his fiancée was with him.

With an effort she smiled in a glassy way at the man who was now asking her opinion of the film, and repeated what she'd already said several times tonight, while her skin prickled with the awareness of Sholto's presence.

The next hour passed in a haze. She smiled and talked and pretended rapt enthusiasm, but the only thing that really interested her was where Sholto was, the only thing that held her attention the sight of his dark head courteously inclined as he listened to someone, the glimpse of an arrogant profile, the occasional sound of his rare laughter that she unerringly singled out from the high-pitched conversation and laughter all about them. He had never laughed so frequently when he was with her.

Ruben had his hand on her waist, guiding her through the crowd towards the buffet that was laid out for the guests. He said something in her ear, and she turned her head, smiled at him, not having heard.

She'd lost sight of Sholto, but as she arrived with her escort at the table they came face to face with him, almost close enough to touch.

For a moment she didn't even notice that Averil was clinging to his arm. All she saw was Sholto's face, his eyes glowing darkly with some banked emotion—perhaps reflecting the faint shock in hers.

Instinctively she made to retreat, but Ruben tightened his arm, tucking her more firmly against him.

Averil broke the silence. 'Hello, Tara!' she said vivaciously. 'I didn't know you were here. Such a crowd, isn't it?'

Wrenching her gaze away from Sholto, Tara summoned some kind of smile and agreed. They were hemmed in against the table by the crush of people, and there was no hope of escape. Averil was looking questioningly at Ruben, who was smiling politely back, and Tara was forced to make introductions, her eyes rising no higher than Sholto's immaculate pleated white shirt front.

'What did you think of the film?' Ruben asked.

'Ruben is the set designer,' Tara explained hastily. Sholto was capable of dispensing some trenchantly damning opinion, and she didn't want Ruben offended.

Averil was impressed. 'Really?' She began to question Ruben eagerly, and Tara, pretending to be drawn to the food laid out on the table, edged away from his confining arm and turned to pick up a plate, randomly choosing savouries and cakes to put on it.

She found Sholto at her side, calmly ignoring her as he took a plate too and placed food on it. Behind them she could hear Averil's light, pretty laugh. Ruben was making a story of the tribulations that had accompanied his search for historically accurate detail.

Looking down at her filled plate, Tara felt nausea churning in her stomach. Hoping that Ruben would eat most of the food, she backed away from the table, her bare arm brushing Sholto's sleeve.

He couldn't have felt it, but his head turned abruptly, his eyes raking her with an almost accusing stare.

'Sorry,' Tara murmured.

'What?' Sholto was still looking at her, but didn't appear to be listening. Maybe he wasn't even seeing her. He had the air of a man who was thinking about something else. He said, 'Where's Derek tonight?'

'I've no idea.'

His mouth moved in a slight grimace. 'Poor bastard.'

Tara gaped a little. 'Derek?'

Impatiently, Sholto shook his head. 'Forget it. We're keeping people from the food.' He moved away from her to his fiancée, and somehow created a passageway of sorts through the crowd. Averil, her hand curled about Sholto's arm, smiled charmingly at Ruben, generously encompassing Tara in the tail end of it, and carried on with what she'd been saying to Ruben, so that it seemed natural for him and Tara to trail after them.

Sholto slanted a glance at his fiancée but Tara couldn't read his expression. Although Tara hung back a bit,

Ruben enthusiastically followed the other two, bearing her with him.

Sholto led them to a relatively quiet corner, and Tara found herself sitting side by side with Averil on an uncomfortably small and hard pseudo-Georgian sofa.

Handing the plate to Ruben, she forced herself to nibble on a tiered sandwich, making it last as long as possible while he chomped through the rest of the fare while expounding on the film industry to Averil, who listened raptly.

Sholto stood politely by looking faintly bored. Tara wondered if he minded being upstaged. But every now and then Averil looked up at him with sparkling eyes, saying, 'Did you know that, Sholto?' or 'That's interesting, isn't it, darling?'

Tara wasn't sure what Averil was trying to achieve, if anything. Perhaps she was genuinely fascinated by the glamour most people perceived in films and filming and the people engaged in making them. Or was she playing some kind of game with Sholto? If so, she ought to be careful. He wasn't a man to play games with. Tara knew that from personal experience.

She shivered, remembering.

Sholto's voice said, with an undercurrent of surprise, 'You're cold?'

The room was large and high-ceilinged, but grossly overcrowded. 'No,' Tara said. 'Of course not.' She hadn't realised he'd been watching her so closely.

Averil turned to her. 'A goose walking over your grave?'

Tara managed a composed smile. 'Maybe that's it. Luckily, I'm not superstitious.'

'No, I suppose you wouldn't wear opals if you were. Unless it's your birthstone?' Averil queried chattily.

'Yes, actually. My birthday *is* in October.'

'It's a lovely necklace.' Averil smiled quickly. 'Was it a gift?'

She wasn't looking at Sholto, but despite the smile and her casual tone, there was an aura of tension about her.

After a moment Tara said in a light, clear voice, 'I sell quite a lot of this sort of thing in my shop. Sometimes I take a fancy to a piece for myself.'

'Sholto said you have a little antique shop. It must be fun.'

'Yes.' Feeling stifled, Tara stood up. 'Excuse me,' she said to no one in particular, 'I'm going to the ladies' room.'

'I'll come too,' Averil said, disconcertingly. 'We won't be long,' she assured the men.

It was much quieter in there. Tara made for a stall, locked the door behind her and leaned her forehead against the cool painted wood. She just needed a few minutes alone. Once they got back she would insist that she wanted to leave.

Unfair to make Ruben leave with her, though. It was a big night for him, and he'd probably planned on staying until the end.

When she unlocked the door and came out, Averil was at the long mirror, reapplying her lipstick. She dropped the gold cylinder into her black velvet evening bag and said, 'I'm glad that you and I can be friendly with each other.'

Friendly? Tara thought. She'd have stopped at *civil* or *polite,* herself. She ought to respond in some fashion, but was unable to think of anything to say.

Averil snapped her bag shut and peered into the mirror, tweaking a strand of pale hair and pressing her newly painted lips together. 'Was it difficult being married to Sholto?'

Tara's breath caught. Could Averil be having second thoughts? 'We're divorced,' she said. 'Doesn't that speak for itself?' She was damned if she was going to play agony aunt to Sholto's wife-to-be.

Looking at their reflections in the mirror, Averil cast her a thoughtful look. 'He wouldn't tell me what went wrong. Except that it was his fault—'

'*His* fault?' That certainly wasn't the impression he'd given Tara.

'—for marrying you when you were too young for it.'

Tara shrugged. 'Perhaps he was right.' If she'd been older she might have found a more mature way to cope with Sholto's betrayal. 'How old are you?'

'Twenty-eight.'

'I was nineteen,' Tara said, 'when we met. I shouldn't worry that history will repeat itself.'

Averil turned at last and faced her. 'I love him,' she said, 'but he can be... difficult, can't he?'

Let me out of here, Tara thought in near-panic. The last thing she wanted was to become Averil's confidante. 'I expect that applies to all men,' she said tritely. 'Shall we go back?'

Without waiting for a reply she headed for the door, almost glad to plunge back into the melee in the outer room.

Two older women now sat on the hard sofa, and Ruben and Sholto stood nearby, chatting in a desultory way.

'I'm developing a headache,' Tara told Ruben quietly. 'Don't let me spoil your evening—I'll get someone to call a taxi.'

Unexpectedly he argued, insisting that he'd come with her, even as a colleague plucked at his sleeve and tried to carry him off to meet a producer whose name made Ruben's eyes light up.

'We'll take you home,' Sholto said, turning from a low-voiced exchange with Averil. 'We've had enough, anyway.'

Across Tara's dismayed objection Averil said, 'I don't want to be out late. I have an early flight call tomorrow. Of course you must come with us.'

Ruben looked relieved. 'That's great,' he said. 'I'll call you tomorrow, Tara.' Seeing that she had no choice unless she was to selfishly drag him away from a possible meeting with an important contact, Tara gave in.

She sat in the back of the car, and Averil turned to ask, 'Where do you live, Tara?'

When Tara told her, she said to Sholto, 'Darling, why don't you drop me off first? It's on the way.'

Sholto didn't turn his head, but Tara had the impression that his shoulders and neck went rigid. 'It's only a few minutes,' he said.

'Yes, but tonight I really need my sleep. Could you—? I'm sure Tara wouldn't object.'

She half turned, and Tara, trapped into agreement, murmured, 'Whatever suits you.'

His voice clipped, Sholto said, 'If you really want that.'

'Thank you.' Despite the restriction of seat belts, Averil managed to snuggle closer to him, her head touching his shoulder. She whispered something that Tara didn't catch, and Sholto inclined his head, laying his cheek briefly against her hair. Tara turned to stare with suddenly burning eyes out at the passing street lights and nearly deserted pavements.

He stopped the car outside a block of flats in a well-lit street of solid bungalows and nicely kept flats, and when he'd opened the door for Averil, she insisted that Tara should take her place in the front seat before allowing Sholto to escort her inside.

It was five minutes before he reappeared, walking rapidly back to the car and snapping the door closed decisively after sliding into the driver's seat.

'I'm sorry about this,' Tara said. 'I would really have preferred to get a cab.'

'I know.' His voice held a harsh note as he started up the engine again.

'It's a long way for you to come back,' she ventured.

'I won't be coming back here tonight. My place is in the centre of the city.'

So they weren't living together. And tonight, at least, Averil had not wanted company in bed. Certainly she had clearly indicated that she was in the mood for sleep and nothing else.

As if she'd asked, Sholto said unemotionally, 'Averil's staying with her parents until the wedding. They have conservative views.'

About living together before marriage, Tara surmised. It had been different for her. Her mother had died when she was barely fifteen and though her father would not have approved if he'd still lived, it had seemed to her that no one would be upset by her decision. She felt a shaft of envy for Averil, because she had parents who cared.

'What do they think of her marrying a divorced man?' she asked.

'Not a lot. But they've been welcoming, for her sake. They're nice people.'

'I'm sure they are.' Averil was a nice person. She said it aloud. 'Averil is, too.' She had been almost too nice tonight.

'I know.'

Of course he did. That was presumably why he'd fallen in love with Averil, asked her to marry him.

'She's very restful,' he added.

Tara lapsed into silence, depression settling blackly on her soul. He could never, she supposed, have found her restful. She'd been at first a responsibility, one he hadn't asked for. Perhaps after that he'd thought her exciting for a while, at least sexually—tempestuous, perhaps. And later? Shrewish, no doubt. He must have been glad to be rid of her in the end.

Absently, her hand went to the pendant at her throat, the silver warmed by her skin.

'Thank you for that,' Sholto said, although his eyes appeared not to have wavered from the road ahead.

'You remember, then?' she said huskily, her hand dropping to her lap. She didn't know why she'd worn the

pendant tonight. For years it had lain in the bottom of
the jewellery box on her dressing table. Well, it had been
perfect for the new dress, she rationalised. 'Averil knew,'
she told him.

After a moment he said, 'It can't be helped. She must
be aware that I would have given you presents. She's a
sensible woman.'

So she wouldn't make a fuss, Tara thought, biting her
lip. Presumably they would both ignore the incident,
pretend that Averil had swallowed the story Tara gave
her.

Her hand lifted again, and she held the pendant lightly,
her thumb caressing the cool stone. She remembered the
night Sholto had given it to her, on her twenty-first
birthday.

They'd gone out to dinner with friends, to celebrate.
Tara had worn a new dress on that occasion, too—a
floaty turquoise chiffon creation that dipped low across
her shoulders and breasts. Sholto had already presented
her with an exquisite little eighteenth-century French
clock that morning, and a huge bouquet of flowers had
arrived in the afternoon. So the pendant had surprised as
well as delighted her, when he told her to close her eyes
and she felt him fasten it about her neck. He'd been
standing behind her, in front of her dressing table mirror, and when she opened her eyes she'd seen the glow of
admiration and desire in his as she fingered the opal,
mesmerised by its deep fire.

'It's lovely!' She'd turned spontaneously to kiss him,
but he held her with his hands on the smooth skin of her
shoulders, while he looked down at the pendant lying just
above the shadow between her breasts.

'I knew it would look wonderful on you,' he said, his
beautiful masculine voice even deeper than usual. One of
his hands drifted across her skin to lift the pendant, and
he bent his head to kiss the spot where it had been, his
mouth open and eager, making her catch her breath

through parted lips, her eyes closing again as her head tipped back.

She'd felt his lips graze along the taut line of her throat, and his breath on her mouth, his knuckles as he still held the pendant pressing against the softness of her breast.

Opening her eyes, she saw him draw back. 'If I start kissing you now,' he said, 'I won't stop there. We're expected at the restaurant. We'd better go.'

Regretfully, he'd realigned the pendant over the place where she could still feel the moist warmth of his kiss. 'Later,' he said, his eyes lingering on it. And he'd dropped a tiny, fleeting kiss on her forehead and moved away, leaving her trembling with sweet anticipation.

At times throughout the meal she'd seen him looking at the opal, and each time her breath quickened, her cheeks flushing at the leaping warmth in his eyes. Afraid of what their friends might read in their faces, she tried to avoid meeting his gaze, but once he sent her a secret, understanding smile, accompanied by a wryly lifted eyebrow.

They'd invited the others back to their place for coffee and liqueurs, and played host and hostess for another hour or so. And when they had at last waved the guests goodbye, and Tara had turned to pick up glasses and cups, Sholto said roughly, 'Leave them. We'll fix it in the morning. I'm taking you to bed, *now!* If we get that far.'

She laughed at him, but before they made it to the bed she'd shed, with Sholto's impatient help, her dress, her shoes, her hairpins, and pulled off his shirt, discarding it on the carpet.

He sat on the bed to remove his shoes and socks, and she raised her arms to undo the catch of the opal pendant.

'Leave it on,' he said huskily. His eyes roved over her body, clothed only in a low-cut strapless satin and lace bra and matching bikini panties. 'I fancy you in nothing

but my necklace. I've been going crazy all night, picturing it. Come here and help me.'

He was fumbling with his belt, and Tara swiftly came
forward, kneeling between his thighs as she helped him
undress completely. Then she let him do the same for her,
and he pulled her with him onto the bed, so that she was
lying on top of him, the pendant trapped between them
as they kissed. Later she lay back against the linen-
covered mattress, while he spread her hair in a wide halo
on the pillow, and centred the opal carefully between her
breasts, then kissed her skin above it, below it and to each
side. And that was only the beginning...

THE CAR came to a halt at a red light, and Tara discovered that she was clutching the pendant in her hand
so hard that it hurt. She was also breathing quickly, and
her skin felt hot, her breasts tingling.

She sank her teeth savagely into her lower lip and deliberately eased her grip on the stone. Sholto was drumming his fingers on the steering wheel. He could have no
idea, thank God, of the direction of her thoughts, the
strength of her memories.

Watching his hands, she saw them stop drumming and
tighten on the leather-covered curve. Heard him take a
rasping breath.

His head began to turn towards her just before the light
changed. A car behind them gave an impatient toot, and
Sholto's eyes whipped back to the road as he pressed the
accelerator.

She stole a glance at his profile and found it austere
and enigmatic.

He probably didn't even remember the night he had
given her the opal.

When he drew up outside her house she was opening
the door almost before he killed the engine. But he came
round anyway and walked with her up the path, waiting
while she found her key.

'It was kind of you to do this,' she said.

He shrugged. 'It's no big sacrifice. You're not afraid to be on your own, after your fright with the burglar?'

'No. I'm not bothered.' She found the key and inserted it in the lock. Perhaps she'd have felt differently if the robbery had been at home.

'They haven't caught him?'

Tara shook her head. 'No. I couldn't give a very good description.' The door swung open and she found the light switch, turning it on. 'Thank you for bringing me home. It was generous of Averil to be so—'

'Trusting?' Sholto suggested mockingly as she searched for an appropriate word. 'It's one of her most attractive characteristics.'

'That must be nice for you.' She hoped her voice didn't betray sarcasm. She hadn't meant it to. Whatever she thought about the wisdom of trusting Sholto, she was determined to keep her opinion to herself in future.

'Nice?' he said. 'It's necessary for me.'

Tara laughed. She couldn't help it.

'Funny, is it?' His voice was a soft snarl.

She found that she was fingering the pendant as though it was a talisman of some sort. 'I think so,' she said. 'In a macabre sort of way.' She paused. 'Averil tried to pump me tonight—about our marriage.'

His shoulders stiffened. 'What did you say to her?'

'Nothing.' Perhaps she should have, but intuition told her that Averil wouldn't have been receptive to a warning. On that thought, something else occurred to her, and she said slowly, 'She's testing you, isn't she?'

'What?'

'She's *testing* you!' Tara repeated. 'She wants to know if you can withstand temptation. That's why she was so keen for you to bring me home alone.'

'Rubbish,' Sholto said coldly.

'Is it? Did you tell her what happened the night you came round here to "talk"?'

'What I told her needn't concern you. That was an aberration—a stupid mistake. It certainly won't happen again.' She saw his nostrils thin as he drew in a breath. And then, before she could say anything in reply to his last speech, he said with positive ferocity, *'Will you stop playing with that damned bauble!'*

Tara's heart thudded in a strange mixture of fear and triumph. Her hand stilled, curled about the pendant. 'Why?' she said softly. 'Does it bother you?'

He didn't answer, his unwilling gaze riveted on her hand. She unclenched her fingers and let her hand drift away, leaving the gleaming stone resting on the quick rise and fall of her breast. The blood thundered in her head. Waves of remembered desire washed over her, and she willed him to raise his eyes and see, respond to her need of him. All the possessive passion that had held her to him after the first time they made love returned in full force, racing through her veins in a hot tide. He was *her* man, and she wanted him.

Abruptly, Sholto moved, swinging away from her, but she swiftly stepped in front of him, breathing his name.

He stopped with scarcely an inch between them. She saw him close his eyes, grit his teeth. *'Get out of my way,'* he said.

'Look at me,' she whispered. 'Please, Sholto.'

He opened his eyes reluctantly, as if he'd been drugged. His face was taut and seemed pale. His gaze moved slowly from the opal pendant to her throat, her parted lips, her eyes. He swallowed, and she saw his mouth take on a savage twist. 'What do you want?' he asked her, his voice losing its velvet texture, rasping as if torn from his reluctant throat. 'This?' His hands clamped on her upper arms and he dragged her against him, his mouth descending in a barbaric, callous kiss that bruised and degraded but was mercifully brief.

She gasped as he lifted his head, but he wasn't finished with her yet. 'This?' he repeated harshly. His mouth was on her throat, burning, pressing against her skin until she felt the edge of his teeth, his tongue searching the hollow at the base. 'Or this?' he muttered, not lifting his head, bending her over his arm as his lips marauded, finding the tender swell of her breast above the black fabric.

He grasped the edges of the dress where it skimmed her shoulders, and she emitted a wordless cry of protest as he yanked the fabric down and she heard the stitching rip before the hook at the top of the zip parted and the zip itself gave way.

Sholto took no notice. His lips, his tongue, explored the exposed flesh, and then his teeth nipped at her, hurting a little, before he straightened, his breathing ragged, and pushed her away from him. 'Is that what you want, Tara?' he asked her again.

She drew a shuddering, gulping breath, unable to answer him. Her hands shook as she pulled at her dress, the light streaming from the passageway behind her making her feel naked, exposed. She was horribly shocked, not only at his unaccustomed violence, but even more so at the fact that despite the deliberate crudeness of his approach, she was fiercely aroused. Baldly, without conscious volition, she said, 'I want *you*.'

His hand moved, she thought at first towards her, but instead it closed hard about the wrought iron railing that protected the short flight of steps. He said, without apparent emotion, 'You slut.' And then he turned again, as if he couldn't bear to look at her any longer, went down the steps and strode away to his car. By the time he started the engine, she was inside the house, leaning back against the door while hot tears poured down her face.

CHAPTER SEVEN

TARA HAD PROMISED to go out with Derek the next day, sailing with some friends of his who owned a large yacht.

She hadn't slept well, but towards dawn she'd dozed off, waking to find it was late, with barely half an hour before he came to call for her. She debated phoning and putting him off, but doing so at the last minute would leave him no time to find another companion, and besides, what was she going to do all day? Mope about and relive the events of last night?

Far better to join a group of people out for a pleasant trip on the harbour, and put Sholto to the back of her mind.

'You're looking a bit wan,' Derek told her as she gathered up a drawstring bag containing sun lotion, swimming gear and a jersey. He wasn't fooled by the tinted foundation and powder blusher she'd used.

'Late night,' she said glibly.

'Ah, the film premiere,' he recalled. 'How was it?'

For a few seconds her mind went totally blank. She could recall nothing at all about the film, and little of the party except her own intense awareness of Sholto's presence. 'It was very good,' she said, trying to sound knowledgeable. 'The acting was splendid.'

In the car she began to remember details, and talked more than usual, making the subject last until they drew up at the marina and made their way to the boat.

Derek's friends had two pre-teen children, and the other members of the party were a husband and wife and their adult niece who was visiting from England.

The children were remarkably competent on the boat, and enjoyed showing Tara the ropes. 'I suppose that's where the term comes from,' she commented to Derek after helping to hoist the sail.

'I guess.' Derek was content to let others do most of the work, though he cheerfully lent a hand whenever extra muscle was required.

The harbour was ruffled only slightly by a breeze that pushed the boat along at a brisk pace. They tacked about, sometimes hailing other yachts or waving back to passengers on the ferries that plied from the downtown wharves to the islands of the Hauraki Gulf.

At lunchtime the yacht hove to off the well-populated island of Waiheke. After a short swim in clear, cool water, the party all went ashore in the dinghy and walked along a white beach to a hotel where they had drinks and lunch.

Later they sailed further around the island and found a pretty cove that they had all to themselves.

The children wanted to explore, scrambling up a steepish cliff among looming trees and tufts of whippy grass. Most of the adults lolled about on the sand, taking advantage of the shade afforded by the trees, but Tara elected to join the younger members of the party.

When they returned everyone else was swimming except for Derek, who lay comfortably propped against a smooth, sandy rock, long tanned legs stretched out before him on a towel, while he turned the pages of a book.

'You're very energetic today,' he commented as Tara approached. Inching over a bit, he patted the towel beside him. 'Have a rest.' The children were already racing to join the others in the water.

Tara sank down beside Derek, and he put down his book to curve an arm loosely about her shoulders, allowing her to rest against him. He said, 'I thought you were tired after your late night.'

'Fresh air,' Tara said vaguely. 'It's woken me up.'

'Hmm. So what's this, then?' He lightly ran a finger along the skin under each of her eyes. 'You've still got blue shadows there.'

'You know me too well,' Tara acknowledged wryly.

'So, tell uncle all about it,' he encouraged her.

Tara shook her head. 'No, I can't.'

After a few moments' silence, he said, 'It's Sholto, isn't it? Since he's been back you've been...different. Like you were after the breakup.'

'Oh, no!'

'Not as bad, but the signs are there. I worry about you, Tara.'

'I know you do. But there's nothing you can do about it, and really, you must stop feeling responsible for me. What happened was entirely my own fault.'

'I helped,' he said simply. 'And maybe Sholto wasn't totally blameless, either.'

'I shouldn't have involved you. It wasn't fair.'

'I've told you, I wanted it. More than you did, actually. Even at the time I was well aware that it didn't really matter to you who I was. Anyone would probably have done.'

'That isn't true!' Tara stiffened, pulling away from him to stare into his face. *Slut*, Sholto had called her. Sensitive to the implication, she showed her distress in her eyes. 'I couldn't have—not with anyone. Only I liked you so much, I thought it would...would be all right.' She'd thought, as much as she was capable of thinking at the time in her befuddled state, that Derek wouldn't despise her afterwards, that he would understand her need.

'I didn't mean to imply you were—indiscriminate,' he said now. 'I was glad it was me you chose. But really the point was that I wasn't Sholto, isn't that so? And perhaps the fact that I *was* his best friend?'

They had never discussed it openly before. Although their friendship had been rebuilt on their shared guilt and regret, the events of five years before had been too painful for them to put it into words. Yet, Tara thought, both of them had probably known somewhere in the recesses of their minds that one day the time would come when they needed to talk about it.

'I don't think I consciously thought about you being his friend,' she said in a low voice. 'It never occurred to me that in trying to hurt him, I was hurting you. And it should have. I was horribly selfish.' She'd been young and muddled and very, very foolish.

'I survived. And, having known him longer, I should have been able to predict how he'd react. Not the forgiving sort, our Sholto. I might have told you that you were playing with fire.'

'He wouldn't even listen,' Tara said huskily. 'Not then, not even later—weeks afterwards. It was as though he'd put a wall between us. There was no way of getting through to him.'

'He learned to do that early, I think.'

'What do you mean?'

Derek hesitated. 'Did he ever tell you what his home was like—his parents?'

'Sholto didn't talk much about his childhood. I know his parents died when he was in his teens.' It was why, she'd thought, he'd been so kind to her after her father's death. He had empathised because he'd been through a similar experience.

Derek glanced at her. 'Did he tell you how they died?'

She thought, not remembering his exact words, only the impression she'd gathered. 'I thought they were in a car crash.'

'Not exactly. His mother died of injuries inflicted by his father.' Ignoring her start of horror, Derek went on, 'Sholto blamed himself.'

'*Why?*'

'I'm not sure. He said it once, and then clammed up. I'm pretty sure his father was in the habit of knocking his mum about. Sholto, too. He arrived at school sometimes with bruises. Then one day when he got home he

found his mother lying on the kitchen floor, battered and
barely conscious.'

'That must have been *horrifying!*'

'Yeah. It was him that called an ambulance, and the
police. But his father went off in the car before they arrived and crashed it into a wall. Died instantly.'

'Deliberately?'

'No idea. He'd been drinking heavily all day. His
mother had a couple of operations and then she was in
and out of hospital for three or four years afterwards.
She finally died of a brain tumour.'

'Sholto never said!' Her voice was hushed, appalled.

'He didn't like to talk about it.'

'I thought he came from a good home!'

'Depends what you call good, doesn't it?' Derek said.
'They weren't terribly short of money. Their house was
nice, all mod cons. But those aren't the important things.'

'No,' Tara agreed. Love and protection were the most
important things for children.

'Anyway, I think he learned survival strategies as a
child. He had a strange ability to distance himself on occasion—it drove the teachers wild. Nothing could reach
him, it was as though he wasn't there.'

'Yes,' Tara said. She knew exactly what he meant.

It had frightened her. Sholto, his face filled with icy
contempt, stood at the bedroom door that he'd closed
with unnatural quiet behind him, while Derek, hastily
scrambling into his clothes, had valiantly tried taking all
the blame on himself, claiming that he'd taken unfair
advantage after Tara, at his instigation, had drunk more
than she was used to, that none of it was her fault, and
that she'd actually tried to send him away...

'Are you telling me you tried to rape my wife?' Sholto
asked then, his voice deadly quiet, but his eyes, turned on
Derek, made the other man stammer into silence.

Her heart thumping in fear, Tara had intervened. *'No!'*
she cried. 'It wasn't like that at all. I... invited Derek in
here. It's all my fault.'

'That's very touching,' Sholto drawled. 'Both the lovers sticking up for each other!'

'We're not lovers,' Tara said.

'Oh? Just a one-off, is it? A quickie while you thought my back was turned?'

'Don't!' she choked. 'Nothing happened, Sholto!'

'Nothing?' His eyes had lingered momentarily on the little heap of cotton lying on the floor that was her crumpled dress, the shoes discarded one by one on the carpet, then travelled with insulting precision from her bare feet up the length of her slim legs to the scanty piece of lace and satin that sat low on her hips, and then on past the flimsy camisole she wore, to her face, which by that time was flaming. 'How disappointing for you. Perhaps you'd like me to leave. Only, as it happens to be my bedroom you've chosen for your roll in the hay—to speak euphemistically—I'm afraid I don't feel inclined to be so tactful.'

Tara looked around wildly and found her favourite floral robe lying over the buttoned brocade tub chair in one corner of the room. She snatched it up and dragged it round her body, tying the sash tightly at her waist. Feeling slightly less at a disadvantage, she said bravely, 'Supposing something *had* happened, do you have any right to throw stones?'

Sholto's mouth thinned. 'We're back to that, are we? Is this some kind of childish revenge? I thought you'd been unbelievably stupid, choosing our bedroom for your little fling, but I suppose that was just an added stimulus. You liked the idea of cheating on me in my own bed, did you?' His lips moved in something dreadfully like a smile.

Derek, fully dressed now, stepped forward and took his arm. 'Sholto—'

Sholto shook him off. 'Touch me again and I'll knock your teeth down your throat,' he said, his tone almost pleasant. His eyes were still on Tara. 'Maybe you were *hoping* I'd walk in on you. Is that what you wanted?

Shocked husband discovers wife in bed with best friend. Sorry I missed the action. But I don't think I'll ask for a replay, thanks. Unless you insist—'

'Look, Sholto—' Derek began.

'Get out,' Sholto interrupted, without looking at him.

Derek looked at Tara, his eyes bothered. 'I can't leave you with—'

'Get—out!' Sholto repeated, his gaze at last swivelling to Derek's face. Tara saw Derek flinch. 'And take her with you.'

'What?' Derek blinked.

'Sholto!' Tara cried despairingly. 'I'm sorry, this was stupid, but we can talk—'

He wheeled, turning his back on her, and flung open the bedroom door. 'Get her out of here,' he said to Derek. And then, his cold gaze chilling her into silence, he told Tara, 'I'll give you ten minutes to pack some clothes. The rest of your belongings will be waiting for you tomorrow.'

'*No!*' It was a cry of pain, but even as she started towards him he shut the door in her face.

Derek caught her arm as she made to reach for the knob. His face white and rigid, he said, 'It's no use, Tara. Nobody can talk to him when he's like this. Get some things together and I'll find you somewhere to stay—'

'I'm not *going* anywhere!' she cried in dismay. 'I can't! He doesn't mean it!' she added, panic-stricken. 'He *can't!*'

Derek said soberly, holding her arms firmly, 'He means it, honey. In his present mood I wouldn't put it past him to bodily throw you out on the street, dressed or not. Come on.' He pushed her gently towards the wardrobe. 'Put some clothes on. Do you have an overnight bag here? You'd better shove some stuff into it . . .'

Tara obeyed at last, shaking so badly she could barely fasten the blouse that was the first thing that came to hand. She hauled on a pair of jeans, and some Brazilian sandals, telling herself this wasn't real.

It didn't feel real, it was like a nightmare, a bad dream from which she was bound to waken. When she'd come into the room with Derek, after sharing a couple of bottles of wine, she'd been feeling warm and muzzy and pleasantly tipsy, and just a little defiant. Now she was rock sober and her body felt tense and shivery.

'I can't go,' she said again, even as, with Derek's urging, she found some undies and dumped them into the bag he held, along with a nightie. 'I've never seen Sholto this way.'

'I have,' Derek said grimly. 'And believe me, you're safer out of it.'

'Safer?' Tara stood hugging her arms about her shaking body, her eyes wide. 'Sholto wouldn't hurt me!' She'd been frightened for Derek's physical safety, yes, but not her own.

Derek just looked at her for a second. 'Do you have something warm to put on?' he asked.

When she didn't answer, he opened a couple of drawers himself, rummaged about and tossed her a sweatshirt. 'Here, this'll do.'

Automatically she caught it and put it on, but said stubbornly, 'Derek, stop it! I can't just walk out with you.'

'You don't have a choice,' he told her. 'There is no way Sholto is going to let you stay tonight. Maybe when he's calmed down—'

'He *is* calm!' she objected. He hadn't even raised his voice. 'I just need to talk to him—' She'd tell him she'd been stupidly drunk, that she hadn't meant any of it, and he'd forgive her. He had to forgive her because he loved her—didn't he?

'He won't listen,' Derek warned her. 'And anyway, I'm not leaving you with him. Not now.'

'But—'

'Where's your toothbrush?' He was walking into the en suite bathroom, holding the overnight bag. 'Is yours the pink one?' he called.

'Oh, *damn* my toothbrush! This is ludicrous—I tell you, I'm staying here!'

Derek came out of the bathroom. 'Okay,' he said almost pityingly. 'Try talking to him, then. I'll wait.' He put the bag down on the floor and leaned against the wall, folding his arms.

Tara cast him a half-despairing, half-exasperated look and went to the door, hesitating a little before opening it.

She walked along the short passageway that led to the large living room, luxuriously carpeted in wall-to-wall mushroom plush pile with a couple of gleaming oriental rugs on top defining the seating areas, one near the big fireplace with its realistic gas-powered fire, the other placed at the bay window that gave a magnificent view of the harbour.

Sholto was by the window, not seated on one of the wide, comfortable armchairs, but standing with a hand in his pocket, gazing out at the blue-green waters of the Waitemata.

He turned as she came into the room, and glanced at his watch.

'Sholto—'

'You're ready?' he asked, his voice remote, his face quite without expression. 'Where's Derek?'

'Sholto, you don't really want me to go—like this. You have to listen to me—'

'Actually, I don't. I'm sorry to disillusion you, but at this moment what I most want in the entire world is to be shot of your presence. I wouldn't trust myself to lay hands on you and physically remove you, but if you don't go, then *I* will leave. And I think you'll agree that it would be rather difficult for you to hold me here against my wishes.'

Tara swallowed. 'You're being unreasonable and unfair. Can't we talk about it?'

'I'm afraid talking about it would be a futile exercise. I'm sure you've convinced yourself that it's my fault I can no longer trust you. In a way you're right. I should have known better than to marry you in the first place—'

'Sholto!'

'It was one of my more major mistakes,' he said calmly. 'But even that can be rectified. I'll see that you're financially looked after.'

Tara thought she was going to faint. He was talking about *divorce!* She looked at him, her lips parting in shock, and saw the face of a stranger—a cold, aloof stranger.

As she stared wordlessly, trembling anew and with ice seeping through her veins, he lifted his voice slightly and called in a peremptory voice, 'Derek!'

Tara heard a movement behind her and Sholto looked over her shoulder, saying, 'Get her out of here, will you? Out of my home and out of my sight.'

Derek's arm came protectively about her, and she walked with him to the door as though walking through water, not taking anything in, even after Derek had tucked her into his car, slinging the bag onto the back seat.

He said something to her that she didn't hear. She should answer him but her tongue seemed to have glued itself to the roof of her mouth. She wasn't even aware of the worried look he cast her way. Some time later he stopped the car and helped her out, and she went obediently where he led her.

He opened a door and drew her inside, and pushed her gently into a chair, then left the room.

He returned after a few minutes with a cup of strong coffee and she drank it absently, without tasting anything, before she looked up into his anxious eyes and said, 'This is your place.'

'You're not fit to be left in a hotel tonight, and I thought you might not want your friends to know that Sholto threw you out. I have a spare room. It's yours for as long as you need it, no strings. I promise not to disturb you.'

'Thank you, Derek,' she whispered, her lips feeling oddly stiff. 'I've been very silly, haven't I?'

'Possibly,' he acknowledged. 'But I've been pretty stupid myself—and maybe Sholto is the biggest idiot of the three of us. At least you and I know how to ac-knowledge our mistakes.'

Tara began to shiver again. 'He said . . . he s-said he does, too. He . . . he—oh, Derek! He wants to divorce me!'

Derek held her while she cried, in great, gulping sobs of despair. He rocked her like a child until she laid her head against his shoulder with a sigh of sheer exhaus-tion. Then he helped her to the bedroom and unpacked for her and left her to get into her nightie and use the bathroom. He brought her aspirin and switched off the light that hurt her reddened, swollen eyes, and left her feeling, if not happier, at least temporarily emptied of emotion.

'YOU'VE BEEN good to me, Derek,' she said now, gazing at the blue expanse of the sea. On this side of the island there was nothing between them and the horizon, a nar-row indigo line dividing the water from the hazy sky. The children and their parents were still in the water, but the other adults were drying off on their towels in the sun.

'I'm very fond of you, Tara,' he said. 'At one time I thought I was in love with you, although I knew even then it was no use.'

Turning a troubled gaze on him, she said, 'In love with me? When?'

'You hadn't guessed? Why do you think I ended up in your bedroom with you that day? I'm not in the habit of seducing my friends' wives, you know. Only, because it was you, I couldn't resist the opportunity. I felt bad about it, but I rationalised that if Sholto was making you so unhappy that you had to turn to me for solace—well, I guess I tried to tell myself he had it coming.'

'It was as much my idea as yours—and the wine had quite a lot to do with it. Not that it's an excuse, but I know I wouldn't have seen that as a solution to anything if I hadn't been maudlin drunk and sorry for myself.'

'I should tell you something,' Derek said.

'What?' She looked at him curiously, struck by a strange note in his voice.

'A lot of women find a sympathetic ear when they're feeling unloved and unwanted very seductive,' he said. 'I have to confess, you were no exception in that respect.'

'Do you mean you deliberately planned to—to—?'

'Get you into bed? It wasn't that cold-blooded. But for some time I'd been fighting a dire attraction to you, the wife of my best friend, and once you started confiding— I guess the automatic reflexes kicked in. I like women, I like to make love to them.'

'I know that,' Tara said softly. 'But you're—selective.' She'd met several of his women friends and they were all mature, attractive, intelligent. His lifestyle was none of her business, but she was glad that he wasn't the sort to prey on those younger and less experienced than himself.

'Thank you,' he said. 'You didn't really know much about men before you married Sholto, did you?'

'I'd dated,' she said, 'ever since I was sixteen.'

'Is that so? And how many of those dates ended up in your bed? Or you in theirs?' he asked shrewdly.

Tara hunched a shoulder. Until she met Sholto, she'd intended to wait until she was married before giving a man access to her body. 'None,' she admitted.

'That's what I figured,' he said. 'When I told Sholto I'd taken advantage of you, it was nothing but the truth.'

'But I—I practically begged you to kiss me.' She flushed, remembering that she'd turned her lips up to him, an irresistible impulse that she hadn't even tried to analyse until later.

'Sure. After I'd been cuddling you, stroking you—'

'Comforting me,' she said. 'You were *comforting* me! I might have been a child.'

'I knew full well you were no child. I wouldn't have touched a child the way I was touching you.' He paused. 'Do you know at what point the comforting became lovemaking?'

Slowly Tara shook her head.

'I do. A long time before you realised it. I was very cautious—I didn't want to frighten you. But I did want to make love to you, I wanted it very badly.'

'I thought,' Tara said haltingly, 'I thought it was because I'd asked you to. I did ask you to take me to the bedroom, didn't I?'

'And I wanted to shout hallelujah. I hadn't dared hope that you'd say it outright. I thought I'd have to suggest it, and I was afraid you'd pull back then.'

'I nearly did. I was horrified to hear myself say it. But you kissed me again, and—'

'And something else entered the equation about then, didn't it?' Derek guessed. 'You were going to push me away, but instead you kissed me back almost angrily. You'd decided it would serve Sholto right, hadn't you?'

Tara gazed down at the sand. 'I guess you're right,' she murmured. 'I was using you, Derek.'

'I knew that. I didn't care. But I should never have tried to make you go through with it. I'm sorry as hell that it wrecked your marriage.'

Tara argued, 'That wasn't what wrecked it. None of it would have happened if our marriage hadn't already been in trouble. If Sholto had been willing to talk, to work through our problems.'

'He's never talked about his problems. Not personal ones. I was the closest friend he had at school, but most of what happened when his parents died I found out from gossip and the newspapers. Sholto never said much about it at all.'

'I wonder if he talks to Averil.'

'His new fiancée? She'd be lucky,' Derek said cynically.

She is, Tara thought, then resolutely pushed the thought away.

Derek said, 'Do you still believe he was unfaithful?'

About to say yes, Tara hesitated. She'd been so sure at the time that ever since she'd regarded it as a given, just tried not to think about it, as she tried not to think about her marriage at all, because it caused too much pain, and no one liked giving themselves pain. 'He didn't really deny it, he just evaded the issue. Said it wasn't even worth discussing.'

Derek gave a little snort. 'Typical. Sholto won't explain himself to anyone. He took the rap for a few things at school that he didn't do, rather than make excuses for himself.'

'I suppose he didn't want to tell tales.'

'I don't think the question of telling tales arose at all. He just wouldn't ever bother to defend himself.' Derek gave a faintly sour grin. 'I think some of the teachers decided it was a deliberate ploy to make them feel guilty. One of them used to get so mad he picked on Sholto every time he got the chance.'

'What did Sholto do?'

'That's the odd thing,' Derek said, frowning. 'I don't think he ever tried to retaliate. He was only a kid then, of course, and what can kids do to teachers who bully them? But...I dunno. It was the teacher who was humiliated in the end. He'd go red and start stuttering with rage. And Sholto would just look at him with a kind of smirk on his mouth—very slight, but *there*. I think it was what the army used to call dumb insolence. Sholto was a master at it. Mind you, it was a different story with other kids. He was known as a fighter. It was one of the things that got him into trouble with the teachers. But in the end all the other kids were scared to take him on.'

'He was that tough?' She could well believe it.

Derek was quiet, brooding. 'There was this day,' he said finally, 'when a bigger guy was looking for a fight and he picked on Sholto.' Derek stopped, shaking his head.

'What happened?'

'Well—the other guy ended up in hospital. If there hadn't been plenty of witnesses to swear he'd started it, Sholto would have been expelled for sure. We had to pull him off in the end. It took half a dozen of us. I think he was out of it, totally—didn't even know what he was doing.'

'H-how old was he, then?'

Derek thought. 'Twelve, maybe thirteen. He was big for his age, though. Well, his dad was a big bloke, guess Sholto takes after him. The other guy was pretty well-known as a bully and a troublemaker, but he didn't stand a chance that day. I think Sholto even shocked himself. It was the only time I saw him thoroughly lose his temper. But...that's why I didn't want to leave you with him the day he . . . found us together. I was scared of what he might do.'

Tara shivered despite the heat of the day. 'That day, before—before we went into the bedroom,' she reminded him, 'you told me that you didn't think it was true, what I said about him. Did you really believe that, or were you trying to make me feel better?'

'Both. For what it's worth, I thought he genuinely loved you. And I don't believe he's the type to cheat on his marriage. He's never been a ladies' man. When we were teenagers most of his dates were foursomes—I'd ask my current girlfriend to find someone to partner him. It wasn't hard to get the girls to agree, he was always a bloody good-looking sod. But he wasn't all that interested in women.'

'No?' It didn't fit with her assumptions. She couldn't keep the doubt from her voice.

'For one thing he had no time,' Derek said. 'He had two paper runs and a part-time job when he was only twelve. In the fourth form, after his father died and his mother wasn't able to work, he cashed in on a craze some of the girls had for making earrings and stuff and offered to sell them on commission to his paper-run customers. Then he started street hawking at weekends, and when his mother died he sold the house and put the money and all his energy into his business. He was too busy for much of a social life.'

By the time he met Tara, Sholto had a successful import-export business, already expanding into Asia, and an expensive modern home that she'd found stark and colourless. With Sholto's indifferent blessing, she had replaced some of the soulless contemporary furnishings, creating a more comfortable, welcoming atmosphere with mellow antique furniture and jewel-toned rugs and cushions.

To her, Sholto had seemed supremely self-confident and sophisticated. She'd taken it as read that his knowledge of women was as thorough as his knowledge of the business world.

She'd met him when he came into her father's surplus goods firm, where she was acting as secretary, and she'd been struck by how handsome he was, with his superbly tailored suit and his unconscious air of power adding something extra. And despite the few words in which he'd told her Mr Greenstreet expected him, she'd responded with deep, immediate pleasure to the distinctive timbre of his voice.

When Tara took some papers that her father asked for into the office, Sholto stood up at her entrance, a courtesy few men offered to a mere secretary. But he hadn't smiled, even when her father introduced them, merely extending a strong, firm hand that briefly closed about hers.

On leaving the office he'd given her a polite nod as he passed her desk, looking mildly surprised when she smiled at him and said, 'Goodbye, Mr Herne.'

He telephoned a week later for an appointment, and before he'd had a chance to tell her who he was she'd greeted him confidently by name.

'You must be good with voices,' he told her.

She was, but his was the only one that had made that much impression on her. 'What time would suit you?'

When he kept the appointment he'd called her by her first name when he thanked her after she'd ushered him into her father's office.

The next time he called, he paused in the doorway between the outer and inner offices on his way out and looked back, saying, 'Harold—perhaps you'd allow me to take you and your wife out to dinner one evening? Tonight, if that suits you?'

Harold Greenstreet looked gratified, and regretful. 'I'm afraid my wife died a couple of years ago. But—'

'I'm sorry to hear that,' Sholto said swiftly. 'In that case, perhaps your daughter might like to accompany you.' He turned to her, and for the first time she saw him smile. It completely changed the austerity of his features and made him momentarily look almost boyish. Tara was still dazedly looking at his mouth when the smile had faded, noticing that the curve of his lower lip was less ruthlessly chiselled than the upper one, the only hint of latent gentleness in his face.

Faintly startled, Harold said, a shade too heartily, 'Thank you, I'm sure we'd enjoy that, wouldn't we, Tara?'

Sholto's eyes met hers, an expression lurking in the dark blue depths that she couldn't read. 'Would you, Tara?' he asked, his voice soft and almost coaxing.

She felt herself blush. She wondered if her father was waiting for her to make some excuse so that he could propose that his current lady friend might take her place, as he'd obviously been going to suggest before Sholto had pre-empted him.

'Thank you,' she said, making an effort to be cool and composed. 'I'll look forward to it.'

Her father didn't seem annoyed. By the time they met
Sholto at the restaurant he'd designated, Harold was apparently enjoying the novel prospect of a night out with
his daughter.

She'd expected Sholto to be accompanied by his wife,
and pictured a very svelte blonde or brunette, with
smooth hair and discreetly glossy make-up, probably tall
and thin, wearing designer clothes. But it appeared there
wasn't a Mrs Herne at all. Tara quietly rejoiced at the
casually imparted information.

Her father did most of the talking, but a couple of
times Tara looked up to find Sholto's eyes on her as he
absently twirled his wine glass or stirred his coffee,
answering her father in polite but general phrases. Several times he addressed her directly, drawing her into the
conversation, and she responded eagerly but was careful
not to talk too much, conscious that the men might have
important business to discuss.

When they parted afterwards he smiled at her again,
and held her hand a moment longer this time as she
thanked him for the evening. On the way home she allowed herself to dream, just a little.

She hadn't seen him again until the day after her
father's death.

She'd tried to contact him that morning, as she'd at-
tempted to contact everyone in her father's appointment
book. Sholto's secretary said he was out of the country
but wouldn't have forgotten the appointment. They'd
had word that his plane was delayed but he expected to
be able to make it to Mr Greenstreet's office. Yes, of
course, she said, she'd tell Mr Herne the news; he would
certainly understand that it might take time to sort matters out, and might she offer her sympathy to the firm?

Tara didn't say that the firm consisted now of herself
and the files she'd kept for her father.

She was answering an incoming call an hour later when
Sholto walked in and smiled at her.

'Thank you for your concern,' she said steadily to the caller. 'Yes, I have your file and we'll get to it just as soon as possible. Yes, I will convey your message to the family. Goodbye.'

The family, she thought bleakly. That meant herself and her father's brother and his wife and three grown children. Fortunately Uncle Al and Aunt Pen, whom she'd hardly seen since she was ten years old, had arrived last night from Palmerston North and taken over at home, helping her with the funeral arrangements. But no one else could be of much use here in the office. She had rather welcomed the chance to keep busy, it helped to hold her together.

Then Sholto smiled at her, walking towards her desk, and said, 'Hello, Tara.' And she put a hand to her eyes and burst into tears.

'HE WASN'T really in love with me,' she told Derek. As he looked about to dispute it, she said, 'Oh, maybe for a short time after we were married he was close to it. I think he was... impressed in some way that other men admired me.' Yet, before she met Sholto she hadn't attracted so very many men. It was something about him, about her blind, headlong love for him, that had given her a glow, an appeal that had never been apparent before. That, and perhaps the fact that Sholto had encouraged her to spend money on herself, to buy expensive clothes that made the best of her shapely though unspectacular figure, and to patronise a good hairdresser who cut and shaped and layered her wayward mop of ringleted curls and showed her how to arrange it in suitable styles.

She'd become a part of his image, she supposed now. An accessory to his business and his social life. 'But when we first started going together,' she said, 'it was because he was sorry for me.'

He'd begun by being casually kind, left with no other choice but extreme callousness in the light of her sudden and unexpected storm of grief.

After a moment's stunned silence, he'd come round the desk and folded her against his chest, and asked her what on earth was the matter. It was some time before she realised he'd come straight from the airport without having received the message she'd left with his office. When she managed to choke out the words, he'd held her closer and waited for the weeping to subside before he said, 'Is there anything more that needs doing here immediately?'

He'd faxed a page of her father's appointment book to his own secretary with instructions to phone the remaining names on it, made two more calls for her himself, and reprogrammed the answering machine in his own voice, suggesting urgent messages could be rerouted through his office, but that owing to Mr Greenstreet's unexpected death, other matters would be attended to in due course. Then he said, 'Come on, Tara, I'm taking you home.'

'He hardly left my side for three days after my father died,' she told Derek. Although he'd refused to sit with the family at the funeral, he'd been there all through the service and the burial, and the gathering at the house afterwards. And he'd been the last to leave. When her uncle had asked if she'd like to come home with him and his wife, to live with them, and she'd shaken her head, Sholto said, 'I'll look after her. I have an obligation to her father. I'd be honoured to fulfil it in his memory.'

He was definitely exaggerating, Tara knew. Her father and he had been business acquaintances, nothing more. If there had been any obligation on either side, she suspected it was probably the other way round.

Harold Greenstreet had been an erratic businessman, indulging in various ventures one after the other, always convinced that the latest would eventually make him rich. Some of them prospered moderately, while others had been financial failures although he'd never had to de-

clare bankruptcy. He'd cut his losses, sell up and move on
to a new town and a new enterprise, establishing his wife
and only child in yet another home, so that Tara had
never put down roots. The Auckland business had lasted
longer than any of the others, and had just about broken
even. Perhaps with the death of his wife and his own en-
croaching middle age Harold had accepted that the elu-
sive fortune he'd pursued all his life would never
materialise.

Certainly in taking on responsibility for Tara, Sholto
could never have sought any financial advantage.

After Sholto's oddly formal little speech, Uncle Al had
cast him a serious, questioning look, and apparently been
satisfied with what he saw. 'We'll keep in touch,' he
promised. 'If you change your mind, Tara, just let us
know.'

'AFTER MY UNCLE and aunt went back to Palmerston
North,' she said, shifting more comfortably against
Derek's willing shoulder, 'I told Sholto I could manage
on my own. I knew I'd leaned on him too much. That
day was the first time he kissed me.'

'He didn't try to take you to bed *then?*' Derek sounded
slightly censorious.

'Oh, no. He came round a lot in the next couple of
months, checking that I was all right. And he helped me
to tidy up Dad's business affairs, and got an agent to find
someone who wanted to take over the firm. I felt too
young and inexperienced to run it myself, I was afraid I'd
get into debt, and anyway I wanted a change. I got a little
bit of money from the sale, not a fortune but enough for
a nest egg.' It had been handy later when she bought the
shop, because she hadn't wanted to use Sholto's money
for it. 'Sholto knew someone who needed a secretary, and
I applied and got the job. And...when I'd begun getting over my father's death, Sholto started taking me out.
We even kissed again several times. But he never stayed
the night.'

Derek said, 'Were you a virgin when you got married?'

Tara shook her head and shifted a little, so that his arm dropped from her shoulder. 'No,' she said briefly, moving her legs and digging her toes into the sand. 'I think I'll have a swim. How about you?'

They ran into the water side by side, and played about for a while. Soon after they came out the skipper decided it was time to go home.

It had been a pleasant day, but she was tired. Too many late nights, perhaps, she thought. Maybe she ought to cut down on them. If the object of accepting all invitations was to stop her thinking of Sholto, the exercise hadn't been particularly successful.

She went to bed early that evening, and again many times over the next several weeks. Andy asked her and Derek to go with him and Jane to a first night at the university theatre and a party afterwards. 'One of the lecturers wrote the play,' Andy told Tara. 'All Jane's university friends will be there. I'll have no one to talk to.'

'Jane—'

'She'll have to talk to *them,* and I'll just be standing round like a big dumb ox. Please, Tara, you've got to come.'

It was moral support he really wanted, she deduced. She explained to Derek and they went along. Andy was quiet, but Jane hung on his arm, collecting interested, envious and sometimes incredulous looks from her women colleagues, and a few sly grins and raised brows from the men that made Tara want to clout them.

The next day was Sunday. Tara slept late, found she was out of milk, and went to the nearest dairy, coming back with a carton of milk and a Sunday paper. She spread the paper on the table as she ate a bowl of cereal, skimming the headlines. *Royal Visit Next Year? Minister Denies Accusation. Missing Man Found in Bush.*

At least there was some good news, then. She glanced at the front page photograph of a grinning man in a plaid shirt, sporting a week-old beard and giving a thumbs-up sign to the photographer.

In the lower corner another headline caught her eye. *New Zealand Crew Die in Fiji.*

She skimmed the item, expecting to read of a boating disaster. Instead, it briefly stated that two New Zealanders had died on a local excursion flight to one of the outer islands when the small plane crashed into a lagoon. All those aboard had been air crew members on a two-day stopover in Fiji. There were three survivors, but—

Tara's eyes leapt quickly to the bottom of the article, where the names of the dead were printed in bold black letters. And immediately stopped there, her head pounding with sudden pressure, her mouth opened in horror. One of the names meant nothing, but the other was appallingly familiar. She read it over again, trying to convince herself she must be mistaken. She wasn't. The second dead crew member was Averil Carolan.

CHAPTER EIGHT

TARA SAT for a time with her mind whirling, then got up and slowly went to the telephone and dialled Chantelle's number.

'I don't want to bother you,' she said. 'I've just read the news about Philip's cousin. Will you please tell him how sorry I am?'

'Yes, I will. Thank you, Tara. Phil's round at her parents' place now, with some of the family. It's a dreadful shock for them.'

'Is ... do you know if Sholto's there, too?'

'He was this morning. I don't know about now.'

'I don't have his new address,' Tara said. 'Could you—?'

'Yes, of course.' Chantelle found it, and Tara wrote it down. 'And here's the phone number,' Chantelle added, reciting it off.

Tara stood looking at the number, biting her lip. A phone call didn't seem enough, and if she phoned first she was sure Sholto would veto a visit.

She remembered the comfort of his arms, of his presence, when she'd lost her father. The least she could do was go and see him.

The address was in a new, inner city apartment block. She took a lift to the second floor, and knocked on a varnished wood door with a peephole in it.

At first she thought no one was home. Perhaps he was still with Averil's parents. She pressed the bellpush by the door and waited. But she was about to turn away when the door was opened and Sholto said, 'Sorry—I was on the phone.'

He hadn't looked through the peephole, because when he saw her his face closed as if a steel shutter had come down. 'What do you want?' he said.

'I just learned about Averil, Sholto. May I come in?'

For a moment she thought he was going to refuse, perhaps shut the door in her face. Then, without any visible change of expression, he swung it wide and gestured for her to enter.

There was a carpeted vestibule, and she waited for him to close the door before walking through a door into a large lounge.

A glance at the decor reminded her of the impersonal surroundings he'd lived in before marrying her. The carpet was pale grey, the walls ice-blue, and all the furniture seemed to be leather, glass and stainless steel. The day was quite warm, but she almost felt goose flesh rising on her skin.

Sholto silently indicated a two-seater sofa, tightly upholstered in black leather. She sat down and studied his face as he stood a few feet away, one hand in a pocket of his sleekly fitting navy pants. His eyes were slightly bloodshot; they seemed more deeply set. His skin had a sallow tinge beneath the habitual tan, and the almost invisible line by his mouth was more pronounced. He looked as though he'd been up all night.

'I'm very sorry,' Tara said quietly.

'Are you?'

It sounded like a challenge, as though he didn't believe her. 'Of course!' she said, shocked. 'Averil was too young to die, and I know you must be feeling—'

'You know nothing about my feelings.'

Tara swallowed a fleeting anger. 'It's been very sudden. I suppose you're still trying to accept—'

Sholto gave a harsh, satirical groan. 'Oh, for God's sake, spare me the conventional sympathy!'

'All right,' she said. 'I know sympathy is inadequate, and maybe you specially don't want mine. But if there is anything I can do for you, Sholto—anything—I wish you'd tell me.'

His face changed. 'Anything? What are you offering me?' he enquired softly.

Tara recoiled, disbelieving, even as his gaze seared her body, leaving her in no doubt what he meant. *'Not that!'* she said, her voice whiplash sharp. 'What the hell do you think I am, Sholto? I wasn't suggesting I should be a stand-in for your fiancée!'

'Weren't you?' His voice taunted.

Tara stood up. 'I thought you might need someone. If you'd really rather be left alone, I'll go,' she said tightly. 'I can see this was a mistake.'

As she made to brush past him his hand on her arm stopped her, turning her to him. 'Wait, Tara.'

She resisted but he didn't let go. Forcing the words out, he said, 'I . . . apologise. I hardly know what I'm saying.'

Tara said immediately, 'It's all right. I understand.'

He dropped his hand, and then raised it to the back of his neck, briefly massaging it. 'You're trying to be kind, I know. It's just that—at the moment everything rubs me the wrong way, and I spent a hell of a morning with Averil's people. I've been wanting to snap and snarl ever since we heard yesterday, but I can't—not at them. You were the first target that presented itself.'

'Grief . . . does strange things to people. I wanted to be with you because I—well, I'm still grateful for the way you stood by me when my father died.' Hastily, she added, 'I know it's not the same thing. But you don't have anyone else, do you? Averil's family will be wrapped in their own grief. I didn't want you to have to bear it alone.'

He gave her a searching look, as if she'd surprised him. 'It was a generous impulse,' he said. 'But the last thing I need right now is you, Tara. In fact, I don't think I could stand it.'

She clamped her teeth together and held her head high. 'I see. I shouldn't have come. But...if you change your mind...if I could help with...'

'I know.' He had both hands in his pockets now. He looked tense, impatient, as if he couldn't wait for her to be gone. 'I'll see you out.'

At the door, as he opened it, she turned to him. 'I suppose you'd prefer me not to come to the funeral?' she asked in brittle tones.

His eyes flickered closed for an instant. His jaw tightened. 'God, no!' he said. 'Not that. Stay away!'

Tara bit her lip. 'All right,' she agreed. 'I'll be thinking of you.'

His frowning glance seemed almost to be one of loathing, so that she shook inwardly, stepping past him. She'd hardly cleared the doorway before he shut the door with a snap behind her.

He hates me, she thought blankly. Why should he hate me so much?

In the lift on the way to the ground floor, the answer came to her. Because he'd loved Averil and Averil was dead, while Tara was still alive. She shuddered. He'd been wishing it was she who had died.

SHE SAW the funeral notice in the newspaper the following day, and decided against sending flowers. Instead, she dispatched a card to Averil's family. They might not even know who she was, but she felt that some mark of recognition was required.

She wondered how Sholto was. Whatever anguish he suffered, she was sure he'd hide it from everyone. His grief would be expressed in private, if he allowed it any expression at all.

Her heart ached for him.

ABOUT A WEEK after the funeral she'd locked up the shop and was walking through the mall with Tod at her side when she paused by Chantelle's florist shop. The door was still open and Chantelle was carrying in the buckets of roses and carnations that stood outside it, tempting customers to come and buy. On impulse, Tara said, 'See you tomorrow, Tod. I'm going to buy some flowers.'

'Yeah, okay.' He went off, quickening his pace. Briefly Tara looked after him with something like affection. She'd been closing up dead on time lately, because since the robbery Tod would never leave until she did. His protective attitude both touched and exasperated her.

She picked up a couple of buckets and carried them into the shop.

'Thanks, Tara.' Chantelle took them from her and stowed them behind the counter. 'Can I do something for you, or is this just a friendly visit?'

'I'd like some flowers. But if you're in a hurry to lock up—'

'No hurry,' Chantelle assured her. 'I've still got some nice red roses left. Special price, as it's the end of the day, and for you.'

'Not red roses,' Tara said unequivocally. 'I think a mixed bouquet.'

'Something festive for a special occasion, or just to brighten you up?'

'No, not festive. They're... for Sholto.' Why make a secret of it, after all? There was nothing wrong with sending her ex-husband flowers as a gesture of sympathy.

Chantelle didn't seem to think there was anything aberrant about it. She said only, 'What a nice thought. Too many people never consider sending flowers to their male friends. But I don't know why not. And about now things will start to really hit him, when the flowers sent for the funeral start dying, and the cards are not coming so often, and people stop calling to express their sympathy.'

'I know,' Tara said, as Chantelle spread a piece of florist's paper and began gathering chrysanthemums, carnations, tiger lilies and partially unfurled gold roses.

She arranged them with some ladder fern and sprays of variegated leaves, her experienced fingers ensuring that every bloom was visible and uncrushed.

'What do you want on the card?' she asked as she expertly secured the green paper about the bouquet, tying it with a discreet purple bow.

'Just "Tara", please.' She couldn't think of a suitable message. The flowers themselves would surely tell Sholto that she was thinking of him, in some small way sharing his grief.

'Are you going to see him?' Chantelle asked.

'No, I thought I'd just send the flowers. I suppose you can't deliver tonight. I'll get a taxi to take them for me.'

'I can drop them in to him on my way home if you like. I'd do it for any customer,' she added as Tara looked doubtful. 'And I could say hello at the same time.'

'Well, thanks. How much do I owe you?'

She waited while Chantelle locked up, and they walked to the car park together. Tara asked, 'Have you or Philip seen Sholto? Do you know how he is?'

'We saw him at the funeral, of course. He looked a bit grim, naturally, but he doesn't show his feelings much, does he? He was a tower of strength to the family. It was he who made most of the funeral arrangements—they were too broken up to cope. Averil was the youngest, you know, and the family still thought of her as their baby. Her mother's distraught.'

'Poor woman,' Tara murmured. 'You haven't seen Sholto since?'

Chantelle shook her head. 'Phil went round the next evening but he said Sholto seemed to have closed himself off. He was perfectly polite and all, but he avoided talking about Averil and he gave Phil the impression he just wanted to be left alone.'

That was Sholto all over, Tara thought. No one must be allowed to see his vulnerable side. If, indeed, he had one.

Of course he did. He'd been in love with Averil, and he must be shattered at her unexpected death. For a few seconds, when Tara had been in his apartment, he'd seemed almost ready to expose his feelings, jolted by the tragedy that had entered his life. He had even tried to explain himself, a rare thing indeed, and apologised for directing his bad temper at her. But then he'd hustled her out, preferring to be on his own.

Chantelle said, 'He doesn't seem to have many friends. There were very few at the funeral, and those who did turn up seemed to be employees. Some of Averil's airline staff formed a guard of honour in their uniforms. It was nice. Of course, Sholto's been living abroad for years. I suppose he's lost touch with his old friends in this country.'

Tara nodded. Sholto had many business acquaintances, but she thought probably the only real friend he'd ever had was Derek, and she'd wrecked that relationship for him.

A piercing regret brought stinging tears to her eyes, and she was glad that a stiff, cold little breeze blowing across the car park gave her an excuse to wipe them with her fingers.

She'd phoned Derek and told him the news, and after a long pause he'd said, 'The poor bloody sod! If only there was something I could do...'

Hesitantly, Tara had said, 'You don't think he'd like to see you?'

'Do *you*?' Derek asked sardonically. And as she didn't answer, he added, 'The only thing he wants from me now is for me to keep out of his way. No, I'll send a card. He can always tear it up if it makes him feel better.'

CHANTELLE SAID, 'Are you okay, Tara?'

'Yes, it's just the wind.' Tara smiled at her as they stopped by Chantelle's car. 'Thanks for delivering the flowers. Maybe... could you phone me and tell me how you think Sholto is?' Hastily, she added, 'I can't help being . . . concerned for him.'

'Yes, I understand. When you've been that close to a person, naturally you still feel something, even if you don't want to be married to them any more. I'll let you know.'

The trouble was, Tara thought, fumbling with the lock of her own car, she would give anything on earth to be still married to Sholto. Despite her certainty that he had never really loved her, despite her conviction that he had betrayed their marriage vows, even despite the brutal ruthlessness with which he had cut her out of his life without any attempt at reconciliation, rejecting all her efforts to communicate, she still loved him. Nothing, it seemed, could ever change that.

WHEN the phone rang after she'd finished a quick evening meal she ran to answer it. 'Hello?' she said breathlessly, expecting to hear Chantelle's light, pretty voice.

Instead a male voice, deep and slow, said, 'Tara?'

Uncertainly, she hesitated. The voice was familiar and yet oddly off-key.

'I want to thank you for the flowers,' Sholto said. 'They're very beautiful. And it's a kind-hearted thought.'

He still sounded different, his voice muffled as though, perhaps, he had a cold.

'Are you all right?' she asked.

Surprisingly, he laughed. 'All right?' he repeated. 'I'm just fine. Hale and hearty and alive. Averil's dead. And Averil doesn't deserve to be. Unlike me, perhaps. There's no justice in this world, is there?'

'Sholto—' This wasn't like him.

'Ignore that,' he said, sounding a shade more like his normal self, but a hint of fuzziness remaining in his voice. 'I'm just rambling—getting maudlin. Self-pity. There's nothing worse. Good night, Tara.'

He put down the receiver and left her holding hers, vague alarm bells ringing distantly in her mind. She'd never heard Sholto in that mood before. Self-pity was the last emotion she had ever associated with him.

What did he mean, he didn't deserve to live? Was he somehow blaming himself for Averil's death?

People did that. When her mother died Tara had been unable to shake the thought that her teenage traumas had exacerbated the unsuspected heart condition that was responsible. Her adolescence, she realised now, had not been particularly turbulent. But like most of her age group she'd had moments of rebellion and resentment, causing tension between her and her parents as she struggled towards adulthood and a new, more equal relationship with them.

She had never had the chance to reach that phase with her mother, nor any time to express her remorse for causing her pain. It had taken a long time for the guilt to dissipate, and lingering regrets still troubled her at times, even though she now understood and was able forgive her adolescent self.

Guilt was a common reaction to bereavement. Guilt and sometimes anger. Was that what Sholto was going through now? She looked at the telephone, paused for several seconds, then dialled his number, getting the engaged signal.

She replaced the receiver and was standing worriedly with her hand on it when the phone rang again, making her jump.

'It's me,' Chantelle said. 'I left your flowers at Sholto's door, but I didn't see him. Sorry.'

'He phoned,' Tara told her, 'to say thank you.'

'Oh, he got them, then. Funny,' Chantelle added thoughtfully, 'I had the feeling he was home but just not answering the door. I could hear music, but then some people leave a radio on when they're out, to deter burglars.'

She was probably right, Tara thought. Sholto had been home but not feeling like having company. He was quite capable of ignoring the doorbell if he didn't want visitors.

Chantelle said, 'How did he seem when he talked to you?'

'Different,' Tara said. 'Depressed, maybe.'

'Are you worried? I could ask Phil to go round. He does have a meeting on tonight, but if he hurries he could leave early.'

'No,' Tara said. 'Don't bother Philip.'

'Of course I don't know him awfully well,' Chantelle said, 'but I can't somehow see Sholto as the type to do anything stupid. Depression is pretty normal in the circumstances, after all.'

But after hanging up Tara dialled Sholto's number again, and got the persistent engaged signal.

He had probably taken the phone off the hook so as not to be disturbed. All the same, after her third try twenty minutes later, she became more and more uneasy. Who knew what a man—even as self-sufficient and solitary a man as Sholto—might do in the throes of unaccustomed grief? Friendless and alone, and deprived with cruel suddenness of the woman who had breached the barriers with which he isolated himself, might he even decide that life was no longer worth living?

She couldn't risk leaving him to it. After dialling one more time, she fetched her bag and a jacket, bundled her hair hastily out of the way with a couple of combs, and grabbed her car keys, almost running as she left the house.

NO ONE answered the bell, which she pushed repeatedly. She knocked a couple of times, then pushed the bell again, keeping her finger on the button. Although she could hear no music, like Chantelle she had the distinct feeling that the flat was not unoccupied. She lowered her head, bringing her lips close to the door jamb, about to call his name, when the door opened so abruptly that she almost fell forward.

'*What the hell are you doing here?*' Sholto demanded as she straightened and stepped inside.

He hadn't turned on the light in the vestibule, but even so she could see that he was unshaven, and his white shirt was crumpled and half open, the sleeves carelessly pushed up so that one was folded to below the elbow, the other above.

At first she couldn't speak for sheer relief. He was here, he was on his feet, and he might look terrible, with hollows about his eyes and a gaunt, pinched appearance, but he didn't seem like a man on the brink of suicide.

Still, she didn't think he ought to be alone, either. 'Shut the door,' she said. And after a moment, when she wondered if he was going to bodily remove her and leave her on the other side of it, he did as she'd suggested, with an air of sullen resignation.

'What do you want?' he asked. 'I've already thanked you for the flowers.'

In the confined space of the vestibule she smelled whisky fumes. She wondered how much he had drunk, and if that accounted for the difference in his voice, the blurred sound of his speech, even more noticeable now than it had been on the phone.

'Chantelle was worried about you,' she hedged, not willing to admit that she'd broken the speed limit to reach him, heart pounding and palms sweating with trepidation.

'Chantelle?' He might never have heard of her.

'Philip's wife—'

'I know that,' he said irritably.

'She delivered the flowers.'

He seemed to be taking a while to comprehend what she was saying, but after a second or two he said, 'What do you mean, worried? She didn't even see me, just left them on the doorstep.'

'That's what worried her. She was sure you were home, but you didn't come to the door.'

He stared at her for a minute, then swung away to stride into the lounge, leaving her to follow him or not. There was one lamp alight on a low, square glass table in a corner, leaving the rest of the room in a dim glow. 'Women,' he said. 'They're incredible.' It didn't sound complimentary. He flung himself down on a sofa near the lamp as though he couldn't stand up much longer, although Tara had been relieved to note that he seemed quite steady on his feet, if a fraction less smoothly coordinated than usual.

As she stood just inside the doorway he made a token effort at levering himself up again. He said grudgingly, waving a hand in the general direction of the chairs, 'Now you're here you'd better sit down.' He cast a glance at the table, and she saw a whisky bottle by the lamp, and a squat crystal glass half filled with amber liquid, but he didn't pick it up.

Tara lowered herself into a chair that was a wide band of leather slung on a metal frame, and found it surprisingly comfortable.

'So,' Sholto said, leaning back, his long legs splayed before him, 'Chantelle sent you round to check on me because I didn't answer my doorbell? Didn't it occur to either of you that I may have just not wanted to be bothered?'

'It did to me,' Tara told him steadily. 'I'm sorry if I'm bothering you, but I thought someone ought to make sure you were all right. If you hadn't left the phone off the hook,' she added somewhat tartly as she saw it sitting on another table in a darker corner, the receiver lying beside it, 'I wouldn't have had to come round.'

'What on earth did you think might have happened to me?' he asked. 'I spoke to you barely an hour or so ago. Less.'

'I got the impression you might have a cold,' she said. *Or might even have been crying,* however fantastic the thought. But she couldn't suggest that to him. 'I realise now,' she added, her voice sharp with relief, 'it's only that you've been drinking.'

'A cold,' he echoed. 'For pity's sake, you mean you came rushing to my side because you thought I might have a *cold?*'

It sounded ridiculous, of course. And so, now that she was here, did the idea that he might have considered killing himself. Nothing, she reminded herself caustically, touched Sholto that deeply. Not even the loss of the woman he had loved and planned to have children by, spend the rest of his life with. Perhaps Averil was well out of it. He might eventually have broken her heart as he had Tara's.

'I thought,' she said stiffly, 'that if you were feeling miserable you might need a friend.'

'A friend.'

The brief monosyllables sounded derogatory, and Tara flared into anger, partly a consequence of relief that after all she'd been panicking about something that hadn't been in the least likely. 'I know you scarcely understand the meaning of the word,' she said. 'But most people value their friends, and rely on them when they're troubled or grieving. And since you've probably driven away all of yours, I could be the nearest to one that you have.'

He said, 'I had a friend once that I valued a great deal. Between the two of you, you taught me exactly how much friendship is worth.' As she whitened, her spine straightening, he added, 'I prefer to rely on my own resources, rather than the uncertainties of so-called friendship.'

'Your resources? Including whisky, I see.' She cast a disparaging glance at the drink by his side.

'Why not? It isn't something I resort to often. In fact I don't remember the last time I got even slightly sloshed. But in times of extreme stress it does have the virtue of taking the edge off certain things. And I'm forgetting my manners,' he said, getting up, but not too fast. She had the feeling that he had to keep still for a moment before he could trust himself to move further. 'Can I get you something?' he asked. 'You don't like whisky, unless your tastes have changed, but there's gin, and wine.'

'No, thanks.'

He said with a hint of impatience, 'Don't be a prude, Tara. If you've come on a mission of mercy you can join me in a drink or two. Isn't it supposed to be bad for anyone to drink alone?'

'I should think you've already had more than one or two,' she guessed.

'So I have,' he agreed. 'But I've no intention of driving tonight, and I'm not even halfway as drunk as I might like to be. Unfortunately I'm not particularly susceptible. Anyway, I promise I won't pass out or throw up if you join me.'

Was that an oblique request for her to stay a while? Perhaps it was the closest Sholto could bring himself to outright asking her to keep him company in his loneliness. 'All right,' she said. 'A gin and tonic.'

He inclined his head ironically and went to a blond wood cabinet that opened to reveal a small refrigerator and drinks shelf. 'Ice?' he asked her.

'Thank you.'

He brought her drink over before subsiding again onto the sofa and picking up his whisky glass.

Tara found the drink cool and pleasantly bitter, if a shade strong.

Neither of them proposed any toasts, and Tara had taken several more sips before Sholto broke the silence.

'You sent a card to Averil's parents.'

'Yes.' Looking at him a little apprehensively, she asked, 'Did you mind?'

'Mind? No. They were very appreciative. Touched.'

'I'm glad.'

'You're different,' he said, 'from the way I remembered you.'

'I've matured. Did you expect me not to have changed?'

Sholto looked down at his glass, nearly empty now, and gently swirled the remains of the whisky in it. He said almost inaudibly, 'I expected never to have to see you again.'

'You can't forgive me, can you?' Tara said, her voice low and shaking with pain.

'Forgiveness,' he said meditatively. 'I don't believe in it.'

Tara drew a quick breath. 'Sholto—that's so...so inflexible. Haven't you ever done anything that you know was wrong? That you were sorry for afterwards?'

'Frequently. But I don't go begging people to forgive me. If it's possible, I set it right. And if not...' He shrugged. 'If not, I just have to live with what I've done. The same way that I have to live with what other people have done.'

She waited, but the silence between them seemed to demand a comment. 'Like me?' she asked flatly.

He looked at her for a moment, stilling the movement of his glass. 'Like anyone,' he said, and lifted the whisky to his lips, finishing it off.

She watched him pour himself another. It was impossible to tell how far down the level of liquid in the bottle was, but he had to tip it quite steeply to fill the glass. She didn't know, of course, if he had started with a full bottle.

'It's a harsh philosophy,' she said.

'You'd rather live by the law of forgiveness, I suppose.' Tara shivered at the note of contempt in his voice. 'That's for people who can't or won't learn from their mistakes. Who keep on doing the same thing, hurting the same person—or people—over and over again, never making any real effort to change, because they know they'll be forgiven, so why bother trying?'

'But it isn't always like that!' Tara protested. 'Surely everyone's entitled to one more chance?'

He looked at her with eyes that seemed to be seeing something else, and gave a short laugh. 'How often have I heard that?' he said. 'A worker in one of my warehouses was found with his fingers in the till. The manager persuaded me to give the man one more chance—they were related in some way, I think the man was his nephew. They both assured me it would never happen again. Within six months he'd cost me several hundred thousand dollars.'

'What did you do then?'

'Called the police and sacked them both. What did you expect? I can't afford the biblical seventy times seven. I'd be bankrupt in no time, and all my employees would be out of work. He wasn't just cheating me, he was cheating his fellow workers, as well.'

'You sacked the manager, too?' Tara enquired. '*Why?* What had he done, except ask you to do an act of kindness?'

'A manager needs to exercise judgement in his choice of workers, among other things. Either his judgement or his loyalty to the company was in question. In other words, he was incapable of doing satisfactorily the job he was paid—and paid rather substantially—to do.'

'But his family—don't you see he had a duty to them, too?'

'When his family pays his salary,' Sholto said cuttingly, 'they can make claims on him to set them up in work.'

The argument seemed unanswerable, but Tara was repulsed by it. 'You gave me a large discount,' she said, 'for no reason except that you were sorry for me.'

'A whim. I couldn't have done that if I'd been working for someone else,' he pointed out. 'There are advantages to owning the company that don't, unfortunately, accrue to the staff.'

Sholto was a hard-headed businessman. She'd always known that, and she had never been revolted by it during their marriage, she reminded herself. Because he had shown a different side of himself to her. A generous, tender and passionate side. The one he had, presumably, presented to Averil. She said, 'What will you do now?'

'Do?'

'You told me you came back to New Zealand because Averil wanted to live here.' Perhaps he would find it too painful to remain without her.

'I've made my arrangements,' he said, 'and I don't want to change them again. Except that we'd planned to buy a house. I'll probably keep this place instead. It's adequate for my needs.'

Tara looked about at the cool, neutral colour scheme, the pricey and rather sterile designer furniture.

When she returned her eyes to Sholto she found a hint of amusement barely curving his mouth. 'You don't approve,' he said.

'It's very... classy,' she said politely. 'I suppose it expresses your personality quite well.'

His eyes sharpened, gleaming. 'Is that a dig at me?'

Tara shook her head. 'Just an observation.'

'Actually, I don't look on my living space as an expression of my personality,' he said.

How typical of him to use the impersonal words 'living space' rather than 'home'. 'Where do you express it, then?' she asked with a touch of sarcasm. 'In your ties?'

He wasn't wearing one at the moment, but his ties had never been flamboyant, even when bright colours and splashy designs were fashionable. They tended to be dark, of excellent quality and discreetly patterned.

The faint smile on his mouth grew. Without answering, he obliquely turned the tables. 'I sometimes wondered if your penchant for surrounding yourself with old things was a result of being moved about so much as a child.'

'Very likely,' she answered. She'd never particularly thought about it herself, but it made some sense. Her father had regarded houses more as investments than places to spend time with his family, and her mother had developed a habit of not accumulating household belongings. Instead of trucking large lots of furniture about the country, they'd often sell most of it before the move.

Tara had always felt unsettled in a new place, usually in an unfamiliar bed in a bare room or surrounded by unrecognisable furniture. She'd had a small collection of rag dolls and stuffed toys that she always packed herself and unpacked first, before her clothes or anything else.

Sholto, she supposed, had never needed such props to comfort him. Recalling what Derek had said about him, she looked at him thoughtfully. If her taste reflected something about her childhood insecurity, perhaps in a different way his did, also. Was his preference for rather comfortless surroundings an indication of his unwillingness to reveal emotion?

'What does that pensive stare mean?' Sholto enquired lazily. But his eyes were guarded, as if he suspected her of some ulterior purpose.

'I've just realised something,' she said. The steely barriers Sholto maintained against the world were a symptom of deep hurts and insecurities, much worse than hers. He was afraid of letting anyone get too close to him in case he got hurt again.

'What?' His gaze had sharpened, the slight glaze that the amount of alcohol he'd been drinking had imparted to them momentarily dissipating.

'Nothing.' He's on the defensive, she thought. Perhaps subconsciously he recognised that she was seeing him more clearly than ever before. And it made him uncomfortable.

During their marriage she'd been too young and too ardently involved with him to even try to analyse his feelings. And at first she'd simply, naïvely, taken it for granted that they matched hers.

After the shattering breakup she'd spent a great deal of energy in a very determined effort not to think about Sholto at all. It wasn't so very surprising that she'd never made any serious effort to figure out why he was the baffling, enigmatic, difficult and iron-hearted man that he appeared to be. Nor to find out what really lay beneath that hard exterior.

'Another drink?' Sholto offered, getting to his feet.

She had forgotten she was cradling an empty glass. Had Sholto just noticed, or was he simply trying to distract her from thoughts that he couldn't read but that made him uneasy?

Tara smiled, and handed him the glass. 'Thank you. But could you go easier on the gin this time? I have to drive home.'

'Do you?'

Her eyes widened as he held them with his. The blue smalt depths held a veiled, smouldering light, but he turned away from her abruptly, leaving her wondering if she'd mistaken his meaning.

Surely, yes. When he handed her the refilled glass he flicked a brief, dispassionate glance at her and resumed his seat on the sofa.

She took a good mouthful of the gin and tonic, welcoming its cooling, steadying flavour.

'All right?' He'd picked up his own glass. It occurred to her that he was emptying it quite slowly now.

'The drink?' she said. 'Thanks, it's fine.'

She made it last. Sholto had lapsed into silence, apparently relaxed against the glabrous black leather of the sofa, his eyes half-closed. She wondered if he was going to sleep. He must have almost finished the bottle of whisky.

She returned to her speculations. At nineteen she'd been dazzled and grateful that Sholto could have fallen in love with her. Perhaps then she had been exactly suited to his needs—not a woman who might have probed his emotions, exposed his secret, inner self, but a credulous, unknowing girl who adored him and saw only what he wanted her to, the confident, successful sophisticate that he was on the surface. And when she began to grow up a little, to ask more of him than he was willing to give, he'd sloughed her off.

Had he revealed himself more fully to Averil? Had she breached the barriers that Tara had never been able to penetrate? Or had Averil been less demanding than Tara, content with what limited closeness Sholto would allow? Was that why he had preferred her, despite the unwilling attraction that he'd still felt for his ex-wife?

Impossible to ask him any of this. He wouldn't give her any answers.

'I should go,' she said quietly as she emptied the glass in her hand.

She got up, surprised at the speed with which Sholto stood too and came over to her, taking the glass from her fingers to place it beside his own on the side table.

As his eyes met hers again, she said, 'Will you be all right, alone?'

Even as she said it she remembered his savage innuendo the last time they'd met, and steeled herself for another knife-thrust.

It didn't come. 'I'll have to get used to it,' he said, 'won't I?'

'Oh, Sholto,' she said, her eyes suddenly shimmering with tears. 'I'm so sorry!'

His voice roughened. 'You've no need to upset yourself on my account. Don't for God's sake start pitying me, Tara! That would be worse than all the rest.'

'It isn't so terrible to be pitied,' she protested. 'And anyway, it's more than that.' She wiped the threatening tears away with her fingers. He didn't want her weeping over him.

He went with her to the door. His hand was on the latch when she turned to him to say softly, 'Good night.'

She put a hand on his arm, and felt its steely rigidity. He was as tense as a stretched wire, she realised, despite the whisky and the apparent slackness of his stance, his shoulders hunched forward, his feet placed apart, and one hand in his pocket.

The light was still off, but she could see he was looking down at her. She leaned forward and briefly pressed her lips to his cheek. 'Take care, Sholto.'

She was drawing back when she heard the quick hiss of his breath, and then his hand snatched at her hair, holding her head tilted to him as his eyes, even in the darkness, blazed. 'God Almighty!' he said, the words escaping through clenched teeth in a muted cry of anguish. 'Why did you do that?'

'Sholto?' Dazed, shocked, she tried to read what was in his face. 'What is it? What have I done?'

'You may well ask,' he said strangely. 'Can you really not know?'

'I don't understand,' she whispered. She was standing close to him, so close she could smell the whisky on his breath, and the scent of his body, and feel the heat of him through her clothes. 'Sholto, I didn't mean—'

'It's too late,' he said. 'Damn you. I can't let you go now. I can't.'

'Sh-Sholto?' Her heart was beating fast, in an uneven rhythm. 'What are you saying?'

'You want the words? *I need you.*' His voice was harsh, as though the words were dragged from him against his will. His hand tightened, buried in the resilient curls. It urged her closer, until their bodies touched, and then his other arm imprisoned her waist, fitting her against him, and his head came down, his cheek pressed tight to hers, his lips hot on the curve of her shoulder. 'You can feel it now, can't you?' he asked, as she began to tremble in his arms. 'I've fought it ever since you walked in the door tonight. I told myself it was despicable, feeling like this.'

'Because of Averil,' Tara whispered.

'I should have thrown you out then, sent you away. I told myself we'd just talk for a little while, that I'd let you

go then. That's what you came for, isn't it? To talk. To
bring me comfort.'

'Yes.' She had one hand on his arm. The other was
against his thudding heart. She hardly dared to move.

'Tara.' She felt his lips on her skin, heard the intake of
his breath, knew he was breathing in her scent—not
bottled perfume but her own unique woman-scent.

His mouth reached her cheek, brushed across it to the
corner of her mouth. 'Tara,' he said. 'You're not fighting me. Why don't you stop me?'

'Could I?' she asked, her voice a bare murmur.

His hand in her hair convulsed. He pulled out the
combs, clumsily, and they dropped silently to the carpeted floor as he raked his fingers into the loosened mass
of curls. 'I don't know,' he said. 'Do you want to?'

Want to stop him? Tara closed her eyes. Her hand
moved from his heart to the opening where his shirt had
parted. 'No,' she whispered, running her fingers over
the warmth of his skin. 'No, Sholto. I don't want to
stop you.'

CHAPTER NINE

SHE TURNED her head very slightly, bringing her mouth to his, and felt his lips open over hers as though he'd been starved for her, wanted to devour her. She tasted whisky, and then nothing but Sholto, felt nothing but him, knew nothing in the whole world but him, his arms, his mouth, his being, nothing but this overwhelming sensation of rightness after long years of deprivation.

Her whole body shook, a wave of heat flooding over her. His lips searched and commanded, and she obeyed, yielding to him in passionate surrender, giving whatever response he demanded of her.

Her breasts tingled, crushed against his chest, and when he moved his pelvis explicitly a dart of fire made her gasp against his mouth, her breath mingling with his.

His hands swept her even closer to him, and she felt with a sense of triumphant surprise that he, too, was shaking. He lifted her off her feet and turned, then backed, his mouth never leaving hers until they entered the bedroom and stood by the bed, when he at last allowed her feet to touch the carpet.

He hauled the blouse she wore out of the waistband of her skirt, tearing at the buttons. But he'd only undone the lower two before his hands were on her skin, pushing the blouse up as if he couldn't wait to get rid of her clothes before touching her.

His fingers encountered her bra, and with an impatient growl in his throat he roughly unfastened it, sliding his hands from her back to her breasts, urgently moving his palms back and forth, creating a delicious friction that she immediately responded to, the tight buds so unbearably stimulated that it almost hurt.

The backs of her knees were against the edge of the bed. Tearing her mouth free of his, she whispered hoarsely, 'Wait, Sholto. Let me...'

His eyes burned into hers, a leaping fire in them, and his forehead shone with a thin film of sweat. The gaunt look had gone from his face—it was flushed and his lips were full and firm. His hands stilled on her breasts, holding them.

'Don't stop!' she said, almost sobbing with need. She arched herself forward, feeling the pressure of his palms increase, and hurriedly finished undoing the blouse, tugged it from her shoulders and shucked off her bra, pulling it out from under his palms.

She heard him say, 'Thank you!' and put her own hands over his, hugging him to her as she sank down on the bed, falling back on the cover with him bending over her, his mouth set in a taut smile.

'You like this, don't you?' he said, but it wasn't really a question. He brought one knee up on the bed, his other leg trapped by her thighs. She began undoing his shirt, flipping the buttons from their holes with unsteady fingers while he caressed her.

He wrenched at the hook of her skirt, then pulled the zip down. She did the same for him, unzipping his trousers, and letting them drop to the floor while he slid his hands under her hips to pull off her skirt and the panties she wore beneath it.

Tara kicked off her shoes, and he bent to remove his, with his socks, then she grasped the band of his underpants and swept them down his legs in a smooth, fast movement.

His eyes, fierce and brilliant with desire, were on her face. 'Spread your hair out for me,' he said.

She lifted her hands under her nape and fanned out her hair so that it lay against the coverlet like a halo.

Sholto stooped and ran his hands up the length of her legs as he kissed her breasts, lifting her feet to the edge of the bed, stroking her thighs and exploring between them. 'You're ready for me,' he said.

'Yes!' She knew he had been ready ever since he'd first pulled her close to him in the vestibule. She looked into his face, knowing her eyes had the same glazed, glittering look of hunger that she saw in his as he scanned her body, proudly displayed for him.

'Like this?' he asked her, his hands firm on her thighs.

'I don't care!' she said recklessly. 'Whatever way you want!'

The huskily spoken words had scarcely left her throat before he entered her in one long, smooth, powerful thrust, and she cried out at the feel of him, hard and hot, filling her so completely, so wonderfully.

He bent further towards her, a frown on his forehead. 'It hurts?'

Frantically she shook her head. 'No! No, it's beautiful!' Already she felt the gathering sensations, the tiny thrills running over her body, getting stronger, focused on that special part of her that was made to receive him like this, in loving, passionate union.

He leaned closer, his forearms resting on the bed, his mouth searching again for hers. 'That's good!' he said, his voice like dark, rich treacle. He moved himself slowly, deeply inside her, and smiled at the sudden tension in her face before he kissed her again, a kiss as intimate as the total intimacy of their bodies.

Her mouth closed over his tongue as she felt her body spasm, all the darting runnels of pleasure coalescing into great star bursts of unbelievable sensation, spinning her in a whirlpool of sensual excitement that went on and on and on—she thought she'd die if it didn't stop, that no one could stand so much delight.

Until she felt Sholto join her, his mouth leaving hers to give voice to his own pleasure, his arms about her, holding her to him, giving himself utterly into her keeping with thrust after thrust into the warm, slick centre of her until he was spent, lying against her breasts while his breath steadied.

Minutes later he said, 'I'm heavy.' He made to move, but she tightened her hands about his neck, silently asking him not to leave her.

'All right,' he breathed on a soft laugh. 'But let me turn us over.'

He accomplished it deftly, even managing to change their position so that his head was cushioned by a pillow and they lay fully on the bed. 'How's that?' he asked her.

'Mm.' She lay now between his thighs, held by his hands cupped over the swelling curves of her behind, her head on his chest. She began gently running a finger down the side of his neck, then over his shoulder, her half-closed eyes seeing how his skin seemed to flinch faintly as if sensitised by her touch.

Intrigued, she put her hand against the flat smoothness of his breastbone and stroked slowly over it, then circled a nipple with her finger, gradually spiralling to the tiny nub at the centre.

Sholto grunted.

'Don't you like that?' she asked him, and gently nipped with her thumb and forefinger.

He groaned. 'You know I like it. You know just how *much* I like it, witch!' His hands began to move over the warm curves where they'd been resting, commencing a series of pleasant forays from her waist to her thighs.

Tara smiled, and shifted until she could touch the little masculine nipple with the tip of her tongue. Already she could feel him harden again within her.

She moved provocatively, and his hands closed tightly for a moment on her flesh, making her gasp, her head lifting so that he could see how he had pleasured her.

His hands slid over her ribs and found her breasts again, his palms warm at the sides, his thumbs burrowing across the softness to encircle hardness.

Tara lifted herself away, allowing him better access, and increasing the pressure between them lower down. For a long time they held each other's eyes, subtly challenging with small, teasing, erotic movements and changes of position, always building the tension, savouring it, deliberately damping it sometimes, remaining still and silent with the only sound in the darkened room their panting, uneven breaths, before cautiously allowing it to build again.

Until Tara, unable to stand it any longer, felt the concentric circles merge and peak, and just before they flared outwards again said commandingly, *'Now!* Stay with me, Sholto! Please, now!'

And the lovely sensations spread and splintered and flowed through her, to the ends of her fingers and toes and back again, while Sholto, his stringent composure completely shattered, shuddered and moaned in the tender, hungry haven of her arms.

Some time later Sholto pushed back the cover and folded down the sheet so that they could slip into the bed, where they lay holding each other before falling into exhausted sleep.

WHEN TARA WOKE at dawn, Sholto was lying on his back and she on her side, snuggled against him, with a hand resting on his chest.

Carefully she raised her head to look at his sleeping face. The lines of strain were erased and the gauntness had gone. He looked relaxed and content, and younger, the way he'd been when they were first married. His lips were parted slightly, and his breathing was deep and even.

She watched him, tempted to kiss him awake, but reluctant to break in on what she suspected might be the first peaceful sleep he'd had in days. After a while she eased herself out of the bed and made her way across the carpet to the built-in wardrobe.

She found a dark red kimono hanging from a hook on the door, and put it on. Then she picked up her discarded clothes, holding her breath as her car keys jingled in the pocket of her skirt, and went to find the bathroom.

She showered, and donned the crumpled clothes, discovered a new toothbrush with the rolls of toilet paper and packets of soap in the cupboard under the basin, and a man's brush that made scant impression on her wildly tossed hair. She had to return to the vestibule to find the ornamental combs lying on the floor where Sholto had dropped them.

After fixing them into her hair she returned to the bedroom, replaced the kimono and folded Sholto's clothes. He stirred, turned in his sleep and frowned a little, then slept on.

Tara went into the living room and picked up the empty glasses they'd left last night, rinsed them in the kitchen and placed the empty whisky bottle in the covered bin sitting by the stove. Then she tiptoed back to the bedroom. It was fully light now, but Sholto's still form didn't stir. The bedclothes moved slightly with his breathing, and all she could see was the dark pelt of his hair.

She glanced at her watch and silently sighed. She needed to go home for a change of clothes before heading for the shop. There was no putting off her departure any longer. Quietly she backed away from the room, and let herself out of the apartment.

TOD FOUND HER rather distracted that morning. A couple of times she said vaguely, 'What?' when she became aware that he was speaking to her, and he patiently repeated what he'd said. Just before lunchtime a customer who'd bought a Venetian glass vase pointed out to her that she'd given him a twenty-dollar note in change instead of a ten.

'I'm sorry, thank you,' she said gratefully, correcting the error.

As he left, Tod gave her a puzzled look and asked, 'Are you all right, Tara?'

'I'm fine, Tod.'

There was no one in the shop now but the two of them. He leaned across the counter and asked, his eyes dancing with mischief, 'Heavy night?'

'Nothing of the kind,' she told him repressively, but the flood of colour in her cheeks gave her away.

Tod straightened, his face reflecting surprise and delight. He said, obviously not believing her, 'If you say so.'

'Have you brought those brass wall plaques down from upstairs yet?' she asked him.

He shook his head.

'While we're not busy, this might be a good time to do it,' Tara suggested.

'Yeah, sure. Okay, boss.' He was grinning as he mounted the narrow stairs. Tara looked after him ruefully. Had it been a lucky guess, a casual bit of teasing that had unexpectedly hit the mark, or did something show in her face? She crossed the shop to look into an old mirror with a gilded frame depicting beribboned cherubs borne on stubby wings. Occasionally she succumbed to the kinky charm of blatant Victorian sentimentalism, and such pieces usually sold quickly.

Except for a perhaps unusual lustre in her eyes, and a faint flush lingering on her cheeks, she was sure she looked quite normal. A soft twisted curl lay against her temple, and she pushed it back impatiently, tucking it in with the others confined by several pins augmenting the combs.

The bells on the door tinkled, and she turned with the welcoming smile she used to greet her customers.

Sholto stood there, his big frame filling the doorway, both hands in the pockets of a black bomber-style leather jacket worn over a white shirt and black pants. He'd shaved this morning, but his hair looked slightly dishevelled, as though he might have forgotten to comb it.

'Sholto!' Tara stepped towards him, and then stopped. He hadn't moved, and his face was immobile, unsmiling.

'I know I drank a lot last night,' he said without any greeting or preamble, 'but I didn't imagine what I think happened, did I?'

'No.' Tara glanced apprehensively towards the stairs, hoping Tod wasn't already on his way down. 'We... we can't discuss it here,' she said urgently, her voice low.

'I don't intend discussing it at all.' He paused there, and Tara found herself holding her breath, a sick feeling beginning to rise in her stomach. 'It won't happen again,' he said. 'That's all I came to say. Except—are you taking precautions?'

'Precautions?' She definitely felt sick. Swallowing painfully, she fought it down.

'Against pregnancy,' he said harshly. 'You needn't worry about anything else, I promise you. I was about to get married, remember?'

Tara shook her head. Nothing like that had entered her mind last night—nor his, obviously. 'I haven't needed to,' she said. 'Not for a long time.' Not since he'd forced her out of his home and ended their marriage. And before that she'd only been taking the pill because he'd believed she was too young for motherhood.

He said something under his breath that she was sure would have been bleeped on TV. 'Let me know if there are consequences,' he ordered.

So he didn't expect to hear from her unless...

Unbearably hurt, and incredulous at his cold, uncaring attitude after what they'd shared only a little more than twelve hours ago, she asked, 'Why?'

'If you're pregnant it concerns both of us,' he said. 'I don't turn my back on my responsibilities.'

Suddenly angry, she said clearly, 'Well, that's new, then!'

Sholto stiffened. 'What do you mean by that?'

'You were quick enough to turn your back five years ago. To end our marriage.'

'Not the same thing, Tara,' he said. 'You'd already destroyed our marriage by your actions.'

'*I* had? Do you think you had nothing to do with it?'

'I think—' He broke off, his eyes lifting to the stairway. 'Come on down,' he said pleasantly. 'The free show's over, I'm afraid.'

Tara turned her head to see Tod moving slowly down the stairs, clutching a large carton. He looked embarrassed, avoiding her eyes.

Sholto said, 'I'm going, anyway. Don't forget,' he added, 'to let me know.'

She watched him stride away. Tod had reached the bottom of the stairs. 'Anything I can do?' he enquired.

'Just get those plaques out and hang some of them up,' Tara said crisply. She didn't know how much he'd heard, but she wasn't intending to add to his knowledge.

SHE SPENT the day alternating between black misery and seething rage. Occasionally she found herself staring blankly at a puzzled customer, or through the shop window, and had to mentally shake herself into awareness. Tod moved about her quietly, as though afraid of shattering her fragile composure. At three o'clock he disappeared for a few minutes and came back with a bag of sandwiches and a bun that he sat her down to in the back room, with a cup of coffee. 'You didn't have lunch,' he said accusingly.

She saw that he was worried, and gave him a wan smile. It was sweet of him to have noticed. 'Thanks, Tod,' she said. 'I'm sorry if I was a bit sharp, earlier.'

Tod grinned, and as the bells announced another customer he turned to the doorway. 'I'll go. You enjoy your break.'

Somehow Tara survived the day. She went home feeling washed out, and stumbled into the house, flung her bag and jacket onto a chair, kicked off her shoes and lay down on the bed.

She closed her eyes, hoping sleep would overcome her, at least for a little while. If she had even a short nap perhaps the thoughts and emotions that had been churning in her head and her heart all day would finally begin to make some sense.

But being on the bed made her remember where she'd woken that morning, and how. With Sholto sleeping beside her, looking as young and contented as he had been on their honeymoon.

He *had* seemed contented then. The rare smile that lit his eyes and softened his mouth had been more frequent in the ten days they'd spent on an island off the coast of Northland. The little house they shared was the only one on the entire island, which belonged to a business acquaintance of Sholto's. They'd been able to swim every day, and lie on the sand in the shade of overhanging trees and shrubs, and fossick in rock pools for anemones and starfish, small red crabs and tiny transparent fish.

Sholto had even spent some time fishing, sitting on a rock that jutted out into the sea and was almost covered at high tide, and trying inexpertly to cast a line that he'd found in the owner's boat shed.

At night, and sometimes during the day, he'd made love to Tara with absorbed attention, devoting himself single-mindedly to discovering what gave her the greatest pleasure. He wanted, he told her one night, to find out all about her, to know every inch of her, so that if he was to see any fragment of a nude photograph of her that had been torn into a hundred pieces, he'd know that it was her body he was looking at.

Tara, only newly awakened to sex, had still been shy with him, and sometimes she protested his minute inspections. But he patiently, tenderly and excitingly wafted aside her inhibitions, so that by the end of their time on the island she would lie acquiescent and smiling while he arranged her hair and her limbs into poses that pleased him, and then stepped back to admire the effect, before coming to lie beside her, touching and kissing in ways that were fresh and strange to her, until her breath came fast from her throat and she'd touch him in turn, to draw him closer and have him hold her tightly and make love to her fully, wholly at last.

The first time, before they were married, when she'd reached out to him because she was lonely and sad and scared and he'd been kind, it had hurt.

Tara hadn't told him that she'd never done this before. She'd been enjoying herself, her skin responding exquisitely to his feathery caresses, her body hot and trembling with wanting him. She hadn't expected real pain, and when it happened she threshed under him and fought it, her mouth crying out against his.

Unusually for him, Sholto had been a little slow to react. She was truly frightened before he withdrew suddenly, his chest heaving and sheened with sweat. As soon as he left her she'd huddled away from him, but he clamped a hand on her arm and turned her onto her back so he could see her face. 'My God!' he breathed. 'Why didn't you tell me?'

'I didn't think... that you'd need to know,' she whispered, trying to keep tears from forming in her eyes. 'I'm sorry. I knew it might hurt a bit, but not like that.'

'It needn't have if you'd warned me,' he said. 'I didn't expect...' His hand absently stroked her arm, soothing her. She was shivering, and he drew the sheet and single blanket over them. They were in her bed, where they had ended up after she invited him in for coffee when he took her home from an evening at the theatre.

'Do you want me to go?' he asked her.

'No! Please, can't we try again?'

He didn't answer for a while, but his hand had wandered from her arm to her midriff and up to her breast, one finger toying with the tight, hard centre. 'Yes,' he said at last. 'We can try again. But you must tell me if anything I do bothers you, okay?'

This time he was slow and gentle, and she realised much later, when she was more experienced, that he had exercised considerable control over his own instincts.

Afterwards she'd hesitantly asked him to stay with her, and it was only over breakfast the next morning that he'd said, his eyes brooding, 'I should have left you at the door last night.'

'Why?' She'd been buttering a piece of toast, but she put down the knife to look at him.

'What happened, shouldn't have,' he said. 'That's why.'

She looked away from him, asking huskily, 'Wasn't it any good for you?'

He gave a sound like choked laughter, becoming a groan. 'It was very good for me,' he said. 'But for you—'

'For me, too,' she said firmly, returning her gaze to him. 'I know the first time was a disaster, but after that— I wanted it never to stop.'

Sholto rubbed a hand briefly over his eyes. 'The thing is, you're very young.'

'Too young for you?'

'If you want to put it that way, yes.'

She looked at him, clear-eyed. 'You didn't think so last night. It's because I was a virgin, isn't it?'

'That's . . . a part of it.'

'Well, I'm not any more, so where's the problem?'

'Don't be smart!' he said sharply, for all the world as though he were a schoolmaster rebuking a recalcitrant pupil. 'If your father was still here, would you have asked me to stay last night?'

Tara shook her head. 'Of course not.'

'I took advantage of you, Tara. That's something no man has a right to be proud of.'

'I don't remember kicking and screaming.'

'That isn't the point! I'm nearly ten years older than you, I knew you were in a vulnerable state since your father's death. In fact,' he added musingly, 'if he'd been around, he'd probably have taken a horsewhip to me.'

Tara giggled, choking it off as she realised how girlish it sounded.

'What's funny?' Sholto enquired dourly.

'I don't think Dad ever owned a horsewhip. He wouldn't even know where to find one.'

Impatiently, Sholto said, 'The fact is—'

'The fact is, my father is dead,' Tara said flatly. 'When he was alive he might have disapproved, but his marriage to my mother wasn't exactly a great example.'

Sholto looked at her narrowly. 'They weren't happy?'

'Oh, I think he was happy enough. He just couldn't stick with one woman. My mother turned a blind eye, but she must have known. I knew before I was twelve years old about Daddy's women. He used me as cover, but I didn't realise it when I was little.'

'Cover?'

'He'd tell my mother he was taking me out for a treat. We went to the pictures, or the zoo. Once we watched the start of a yacht race. Anything that was a legitimate excuse for an outing.'

'Your mother didn't go with you?'

'Sometimes, but she was always tired. She was a true housewife, everything had to be cleaned and polished every week. She worked hard, and on Saturday afternoon she liked to nap. No one knew that she had a weak heart. She was glad to see Dad taking me out; it gave her a chance to rest, and I suppose she thought as long as I was with him he couldn't be getting up to anything. But sometimes we only stayed for an hour or so at the zoo or whatever event we'd attended. Then he'd buy me an ice-cream and a bag of chips, and a kid's magazine or a comic book, and slip into a house while I sat in the car.'

'The same house, always?'

'For a few months at a time. After a while it would change to a different one. He said not to tell Mum because she didn't approve of my snacking between meals. When I was about ten I dimly realised he was actually bribing me, and I started blackmailing him for things I wanted. That's how I got my first bike.'

Sholto laughed quietly. 'You little devil!'

'But that didn't last long,' she confessed with a wry answering smile, 'because he guessed that I was getting too old to be fooled, and he stopped taking me out.'

'It was a case of do as I say, not as I do?'

'Exactly. So I wouldn't worry about what he would have said if he knew. He had no right to judge.'

'It isn't actually your father's judgement I'm concerned with.'

'Well, there's no one else to be bothered about me sleeping with you.'

'There's me,' he said. He looked faintly disgusted with himself. 'I promised your uncle I'd look after you.'

'You have. You did that beautifully, last night, too.'

Sholto shook his head. But his sombre self-contempt hadn't stopped him from sharing her bed again and again. Nor from taking her, eventually, to his. And it was after their first night together in his stark, high-tech house that he'd asked her to marry him.

How BLIND she'd been, to everything but her young, full-flowering love for him. Mistaking his male passion, his near-obsession with her on a physical level, for love, she'd revelled in the novelty of being Sholto's wife, and seen a rosy future stretching before them.

The first small shock had been when he'd vetoed her coming off the pill once they were married. 'It's enough that I've tied you down to a marriage at your age, without adding a family as well. Wait a few years. You'll still be able to have babies when you're twenty-five.'

Besotted, and used to allowing Sholto to make decisions for her since her father's death, she'd quelled her disappointment and obeyed. Looking back, it had been unfair to accuse him of deliberately controlling her life. He hadn't needed to exercise any coercion because she'd been only too willing to let him take her over. Maybe she'd subconsciously treated him in some ways as a replacement father, looking to him for all the security and certainty she'd missed not only since Harold's death but throughout her childhood.

For over a year she'd lived in a halcyon world where everything was bright and shining and new and wonderful. She didn't remember now when unease set in, when she began to feel that Sholto was spending more and more of his time away from her. Perhaps it was when she'd finished transforming his house into a comfortable and inviting place, a home where it felt all right to kick off your shoes and put your feet up on the coffee table or throw a few cushions on the rug and lie there to read a book or magazine, where in the evenings she could snuggle up to Sholto on a big, invitingly soft sofa that was long enough to accommodate his length, and broad enough for both of them to lie on if they were too eager for each other to repair to the bedroom.

Or had it been when he was creating the Hong Kong branch of the business? She had accompanied him on his first visit, but had spent much of her time alone while he made and kept appointments with officials and business contacts. Although disappointed that they hadn't had a lot of time together, she didn't think she'd complained much. But the next time Sholto had said, 'It wasn't a lot of fun for you, and I don't like the idea of you being on your own so much in that place, anyway. Wait until I've got the business sorted out, and we'll take a proper holiday.'

That vague future had never materialised. The expanding business seemed to take more and more of his time. And Tara had begun to occupy herself as a casual consultant in home decorating and a scout for people who wanted particular items of furniture, especially antiques, but didn't have the time to hunt for themselves. It had begun as a favour for friends, but soon she was working for others who'd heard of her skills and were willing to pay for such services.

She didn't know until he dropped a casual remark that sometimes Sholto's secretary went along on his business trips.

'You didn't tell me that!' she'd said sharply.

Looking mildly surprised, Sholto said, 'You never asked. It's no secret.'

He'd introduced her to his secretary just before their marriage. A middle-aged widow, she had been at their wedding, one of the few guests that Sholto had invited.

Tara's aunt and uncle and cousins had been there, and her mother's sister had surprised her by flying over from Australia for the occasion with her husband. A few of her friends came, a couple of them already married themselves—one with a baby—and her neighbours who, since her mother's death, had shown kindly concern for the bereft teenager and her father. There were people from her father's office building, and some from her tennis club and from the night school where she'd studied conversational Japanese. Derek had stood at Sholto's side, and Tara's cousin had been bridesmaid.

She needn't be jealous of Sholto's secretary, she'd assured herself, remembering the stocky, motherly figure of the woman who had been the first to congratulate her employer outside the church after their wedding. But when she made one of her rare visits to his business premises she was considerably surprised to find a much younger, extremely pretty brunette ensconced in the outer office.

Her chagrin was increased by the young woman's determination to establish Tara's credentials before allowing her to see Sholto. When at last she was shown in, she questioned Sholto with annoyance in her voice, and he answered curtly that Mrs Drinner had left some time ago, taking early retirement to go and live with her daughter in Timaru.

'If I'd known you needed a new secretary,' Tara said, her voice almost accusing, '*I* could have done the job. Did you think of that?'

'It wouldn't be a good idea.'

'Why not?'

'Because you're my wife,' he said, 'not my secretary. It would never work.'

'How do you know? You've never tried it.'

'Look, I have a busy schedule today. What are you here for, Tara?'

She'd stormed out of the office, telling him not to bother. She'd been hoping they might have lunch together, but there was no point now, they'd only row.

At least *she* would have. Sholto, she soon discovered, simply deflected every shaft she threw in anger and refused to be drawn into an argument. When she tackled the subject again he said flatly, 'Janette was the applicant with the best qualifications, she does the job well. I have no interest in her other than that. There is nothing more to say.' And then he simply walked away.

That night when he reached for her after they went to bed, she'd been stiff and cold at first, nearly rebuffing him, except that she needed the reassurance of being close to him, of knowing that he desired her. It hadn't been long before her resistance and her jealousy disappeared under the skill of his lovemaking, to return faintly when he left for his office the following day.

She'd told herself not to be silly, that Sholto loved her and only her. But much later, examining the events of the past, she could see that it was then that she had begun to distrust him.

CHAPTER TEN

TARA STIRRED restlessly on the bed, and with a sigh got to her feet. She'd make herself eat something, then go for a walk. The exercise might help her to sleep when she went to bed properly.

But even as she set out at a brisk pace some time later, thoughts, memories, came crowding into her mind.

In retrospect she supposed it was sex that had held their marriage together for the short time it had lasted. At first she'd been content with that and the feeling Sholto had given her of being cherished and admired, and they had soon discovered that they liked similar music and films, enjoyed long walks, and could talk amicably on what Tara came to think of as dinner-table topics.

Sholto never discussed his feelings, and she had soon stopped talking about her emotions, because it was so one-sided that she began to feel foolish about pouring out her heart to him.

She was pleased that he liked her to entertain for him, although apart from Derek the only people he asked to the house were business contacts rather than friends. At some stage, she recalled, she had realised guiltily that she scarcely saw her own friends any more, for Sholto had filled her life and her heart so completely.

She suggested they could have a party, and asked all her old friends. With her encouragement a few of them began to call again casually, or she would invite them for a meal. Sholto was unfailingly polite, but before long their visits became less frequent. The combination of the palatial house and Sholto's cool and distant courtesy made them uncomfortable.

When Tara accused him of driving her friends away, he raised his brows and said, 'I've never objected to you having your friends here.'

'You don't really want them.'

'They're your friends, Tara. They come to see you.'

'But Sholto, don't you *like* them? Any of them?' she asked, perplexed.

'I don't dislike them.'

Most of them were younger than Sholto, she reminded herself. He couldn't be blamed for not relating to them. She began meeting them at other places, in town or at their homes. Sholto didn't mind. If anything, he was probably relieved.

When had she become convinced that Sholto was unfaithful? The small clues had built up so gradually she wasn't even sure.

She'd found the outer office deserted one day when she dropped in unexpectedly at his office. Pushing open the connecting door, she found Sholto and his new secretary side by side, their dark heads almost touching as they studied some papers laid before them on the desk.

'Am I interrupting?' she asked, a little too loudly.

Sholto straightened quickly and said, 'Yes, but we've nearly finished. You could start typing it up now, Janette.'

Janette hadn't smiled as she gathered up the papers into a folder and walked past Tara with a frosty, 'Good morning, Mrs Herne.'

Usually Sholto greeted Tara with a kiss, but today he didn't come out from behind his desk, perhaps conscious of his secretary's presence in the outer room. She hadn't closed the door. 'What do you want, Tara?' he enquired. 'I've a pretty busy morning, I'm afraid.'

Several years later Tara didn't remember why she'd called in that day—perhaps just on impulse, out of a desire to see him and talk to him. But she remembered with hurtful clarity the disappointment when it seemed that he had no time for her, her sense of rejection.

TONIGHT SHE'D walked further than usual, and by the time she turned for home it was getting dark. She didn't realise until she reached the beginning of her street and swept the empty road with her eyes that she'd been half-hoping she'd find Sholto awaiting her again, as he had once before.

She had, she acknowledged now, been too young for marriage, as Sholto had said. She had been unwilling to accept that the first flush of love would inevitably fade, and that everyday life sometimes had to take precedence over romance.

Sometimes, she admitted, she'd been inclined to sulk when they'd been invited out to some function, only to have Sholto plead inability to join her due to his business commitments. Even now she suspected that he'd invented excuses, though he'd always urged her not to miss anything on his account. One rather tense discussion took place while Derek was visiting, and when he offered to accompany her in Sholto's stead to a black-tie affair, Sholto seconded the notion immediately, obviously glad to be let off the hook.

For some reason which at the time she hadn't even tried to examine Tara had for several months attended a great many parties, shows and dinners that ultimately bored her. But she'd never admitted her lack of enjoyment to Sholto. When he asked, she'd launch into an animated account of how exciting the event had been. She casually dropped the names of men she had talked to, danced with, sat next to. All perfectly innocent encounters, and anyway, Sholto was still the only man she was interested in.

'Trying to get his attention,' she murmured now as she made herself a warm chocolate drink before going to bed. 'Pathetic.' How immature she had been.

He would listen without a blink, but sometimes there was an edge to his lovemaking later that both excited and frightened her, as though she was flirting with some unknown and half-recognised danger.

Leaning back on the kitchen counter, she seriously and systematically analysed her own behaviour in those months. She'd been trying to spark some emotional reaction from Sholto. Going about it blindly, clumsily. The lack of real communication in their marriage hadn't been her fault, to start with. But the way she'd tried to rectify it had inevitably made matters worse. If Sholto was disturbed, the only way he'd shown it was to retreat further and further behind that impregnable wall with which he shut out the world.

Tonight, Tara recognised, there was no escaping the memories. She'd never taken a sleeping pill in her life, but as she lay wakeful despite feeling dead tired mentally and physically, she wished she had one in the house.

Looking back at her younger self, she saw how deeply frightened she'd been at the increasing emotional distance between her and Sholto. She'd first accused him of loving his business more than he did her. The more she shouted and wept the more time he spent at his office, and gradually she began to suspect that it wasn't only work that kept him away. Several more times she had called without warning at the office, narrowly observing his dealings with his secretary.

'Janette's in love with you, you know,' she told him with apparent carelessness one night as they got ready for bed. She was unpinning her hair, because in the early days of their marriage Sholto had said that he liked her to leave it loose at night.

'Don't be silly,' Sholto replied curtly. 'You're imagining things.'

'She blushed when you spoke to her this afternoon.'

'I speak to her dozens of times a day. If she blushed it was because you were there. You make her nervous.'

'Why should I make her nervous?'

Sholto shrugged. 'You don't seem to like her much.'

'I don't dislike her,' Tara said, echoing his lukewarm remark about her friends. 'I'm always perfectly nice to her.' She was, too. They were dreadfully polite to each other, she and Janette.

'You should let her go,' she advised. 'It's not fair to keep her on a string.'

'I'm not keeping her on a string,' Sholto said impatiently. 'And I won't sack a perfectly good secretary because of some bee you have in your bonnet.' He turned out the centre light and got into bed.

'I don't have a bee in my bonnet. It's true.' Tara slid into the bed beside him.

'You've asked her, have you?' he enquired sarcastically.

'Of course not. But women can sense these things.'

Sholto laughed derisively, turning to douse the bedside light. When he made to draw her to his side, Tara resisted, offended at his offhand dismissal of her theory. He released her and lay back on his pillow. 'You don't need to fight me,' he said rather wearily. 'Just tell me if you don't want me tonight.'

She did want him, but she wanted to talk this out first. Only Sholto wouldn't talk. She began to feel like a shrew, and in the end turned her back to him and humped the sheet and blanket over her shoulder, pointedly pretending to sleep.

From being convinced that Janette was in love with Sholto, it was an easy step to deducing that he was being less than honest when he professed not to know it. And from there it had seemed an inevitable conclusion that they were having an affair.

And had they? Reviewing the evidence, Tara saw that it had not been nearly as conclusive as she'd thought then. Hearing part of a telephone conversation that to her had seemed furtive, Sholto ringing off after he'd seen her standing in the doorway when he'd probably thought she was in the bath. His surprised stare at her query,

'Who was that?' His noncommittal reply of, 'Just business'. A faint feminine scent that hung about his suit when he claimed to have been meeting with a group of manufacturers all day. She hadn't even asked him if any of them were women. A birthday card from Janette displayed on his desk. Hearing them laughing as she came into his office, both sobering abruptly at her entrance. Even the fact that he didn't make love to her so often, although in hindsight she knew that she'd increasingly repulsed his first advances, pretending reluctance, forcing him to woo her anew each time. And then the night she'd come home early from a party with an upset stomach and found that Sholto, who'd said he'd work for a while in his home office and then have an early night because he had a morning flight next day to Hong Kong, wasn't there.

'I was at Janette's,' he said, surprised to see her on his return later that evening.

'Why?'

He'd looked rather displeased but answered readily enough. 'I found a mistake in one of the documents I'm taking with me tomorrow.'

'What sort of mistake?'

He paused before replying briefly, 'Missing paragraphs.'

'You could have phoned her.'

'She offered to retype it at home if I took it over. I would have left a note if I hadn't thought I'd be back long before you got home. Didn't you enjoy the party?'

'I was feeling sick. Something I ate. How long have you been out for?'

This time his answer was decidedly irritated. 'About half an hour. What does it matter?' He leaned over and turned on the bedside light. 'You look a bit pale. Can I get you anything? Maybe I should call a doctor.'

His concern had made her feel a little better, but the next day she wondered if it had been calculated to distract her from questioning him further about his unexpected absence.

She began wondering about other times when she'd left him at home alone. And about all kinds of small incidents that suddenly acquired sinister significance. Until one day she'd found herself flinging the accusation in his face. 'I know you're sleeping with Janette!' she'd screamed at him. 'What sort of idiot do you think I am?'

For a moment she'd thought he wasn't going to react at all. His face was a mask, rigid and unreadable. Then he'd said flatly, 'If you believe that, you *are* an idiot.' And he'd turned from her, walking away.

Tara, furious and upset, had followed. She'd called him names, not only him but Janette, too, growing more certain when with cold anger he told her to curb her tongue. Accused him of things that even she didn't really believe, demanded to know who else he'd been sleeping with. Was Janette privileged, or did he have a woman in every port—in Auckland, Hong Kong, Sydney?

'The only woman I'm sleeping with is you,' he told her.

'You're lying!' Citing the growing amount of time he spent away from her either at work or overseas, his indifference to what she did, whether he was away or at home, his reluctance to join in her activities, the time he spent with Janette and the fact that he'd 'sneaked off to be with her' at least once in Tara's absence, she challenged him to disprove her suspicions.

Sholto, of course, had simply refused to respond in any way. She had ultimately exhausted herself, battering at the stone wall of his indifference to her tantrum. And Sholto offered no further explanations. As far as he was concerned, she either took his word or she didn't.

In the end he'd left the house, and she'd cried herself to sleep, wondering if he was with Janette now.

He hadn't come home that night, and the next day she'd hovered near the phone, sometimes lifting the receiver to call his office, each time losing her nerve before she dialled.

She thought about going to see him, and had called a taxi, intending to confront him in his office. Assuming that was where he would be.

Halfway there she had changed her mind. Not only Sholto, but Janette would be there. Janette with her cool 'Good afternoon, Mrs Herne,' that mocked her. And her 'I'll ask if Mr Herne is free to see you.' And her covert, yearning looks at Sholto that he claimed never to have noticed. Janette, who always looked as though she'd recently been cleaned and polished, her smooth dark hair like varnished mahogany, her make-up perfect, her creaseless, understated office suits managing to look smart, businesslike and sexy at the same time.

Tara's eyes still felt puffy and sore from her crying binge the previous night, and when she'd paused at the dressing table to bundle her hair up and skewer it into some kind of submission with pins, the mirror had shown her a wan, colourless face with blotchy pink patches on the cheekbones. Not caring what she wore when she got up, she'd thrown on a cheap cotton frock bought at a sale before she was married, and hadn't bothered to change, only grabbing a jacket and her purse before she left the house.

She leaned forward, saying to the driver, 'I'm sorry, I've changed my mind.'

He slowed the cab, a long-suffering expression on his face. 'So where do you want to go, then?' he asked her grumpily.

About to tell him, 'Back home,' she saw that they were approaching the street where Derek had his office. 'Turn left at the next corner,' she instructed.

Derek was surprised to see her when his secretary ushered her in, but he smiled questioningly, dropped the pen he was using and stood up to take her hand, kissing her cheek. 'This is an unexpected pleasure,' he said. 'What can I do for you, Tara?'

She started to speak, then found tears welling again in her eyes.

Derek made a soft exclamation and took her in his arms.

When she'd regained control, he said, 'Is it Sholto? He's not . . . hurt, or anything?'

'Yes,' she said. 'I mean, no, he's not hurt. Derek, you know him better than anyone. What would you say if I told you he'd been unfaithful to me?'

'I'd say it's unlikely,' Derek said slowly. 'What makes you think that, Tara?'

'Well, he—' But it seemed wrong to be laying her complaints about her husband before his best friend. Cataloguing the evidence would be sordid and demeaning. 'He has,' she said defiantly. 'I know it. I was going to see him, because last night he—he walked out and didn't come home. But—well, I changed my mind, and I asked the taxi driver to drop me here because I needed to talk to someone and you've always been good to me, but—I'm sorry, I shouldn't have involved you in this. I'd better go.'

Derek insisted on taking her home in his own car, and she'd not been able to resist comparing his instantly abandoning his unfinished work with Sholto's frequent claims that he couldn't neglect his work to be with her. And once there Derek hadn't left her to her own devices, but had made her sit down and, telling her she needed something to buck her up, raided the drinks cabinet, coming up with a bottle of champagne.

'The best pick-me-up ever invented,' he told her. He'd even made her smile after a glass or two, with gentle jokes. But after the third glass she'd begun crying again, and he'd looked at first horrified and then rueful, before moving to sit beside her and pull her into his arms again, saying, 'Maybe champagne wasn't such a great idea after all.'

'Yes, it was,' she sobbed, clinging to him. 'You've been wonderful to me, Derek, I'm so glad you're here.'

Do you know, Derek had asked her that day they had sat on the beach, *at what point the comforting became lovemaking?*

She still didn't know, but she had become gradually aware that some line had been crossed. And made only a feeble effort to draw back from it. If Sholto didn't want her, at least someone did. Derek was not only kind and understanding and nice, he was also a connoisseur of women.

'In other words,' Tara said to herself years later, speaking into the darkness of her bedroom, 'he was good for your ego.'

She could still scarcely believe that she'd actually invited Derek into her bedroom—hers and Sholto's. 'I must have been mad,' she decided. Perhaps Sholto had been right when he said that somewhere at the back of her mind was a bizarre hope that he'd interrupt them.

But when he had, the consequences had been much more drastic than she could ever have imagined.

AT SOME STAGE in the long night she fell asleep, and woke feeling calmer than she had since Sholto had come back. For years she'd been repressing her memories, her feelings about their marriage, unable to analyse what had gone awry without anger and grief distorting her thinking.

What had seemed damning at the time amounted, after all, to very circumstantial evidence indeed when seen objectively at a distance of several years.

The one factor that had some possible foundation was her assessment of Janette's feelings for her boss. Deep within she remained convinced that, in that at least, she had not been imagining things. Sholto was a dynamic, handsome man, and his secretary might well have been attracted to him. But, Tara conceded, nothing in Janette's strictly professional manner had given away any such emotion.

Even if Tara's instinct had been right, her reactions had been hasty, overwrought and, she confessed to herself, plain wrong.

Last night she'd learnt some unpleasant things about herself. Looking back at her younger self was almost like examining the life of a stranger, or studying a character in a book or a film. As for Sholto, the thought of him was like a hollow void, a great empty space in her heart, not so much painful as simply unnatural, as if she were suffering from a chronic condition that wasn't visible on the outside but that inwardly maimed her, so that she was aware of being somehow incomplete. Sometimes she felt hardly real at all.

PAINFULLY, over several weeks, Tara reconciled herself to the fact that she had lost Sholto forever. Whatever need he'd had of her the night he'd taken her in such a frenzy of passion to his bed, he'd evidently assuaged it. Perhaps it wasn't her he needed so much as some means to blot out for a time the memory of Averil and how she had died. Perhaps any woman would have done. Perhaps he'd been too drunk to care.

Certainly he'd regretted it in the morning. Regretted it, and hated himself for what he'd done, hated Tara even more because he had made love to her, and so betrayed Averil's memory.

'WILL YOU be able to help with the children's picnic this year?' Chantelle asked Tara. They were having a quick late lunch together in the mall coffee shop. 'We're taking them to Wenderholm.'

Tara laughed. 'I might have known you had an ulterior motive in suggesting lunch.'

'Not at all.' Chantelle grinned. 'I could have just popped into Bygones and asked you. I wanted the pleasure of your company.' She looked at Tara rather searchingly and said, more seriously, 'Besides, you've been looking a bit under the weather. Have you been skipping meals?'

'Not many,' Tara answered. She hadn't been very hungry lately. 'It's just that the end of the year is coming up. You know how busy we get.'

'Mm, but you don't look so pale and thin every year. Sholto asked me how you were, and when I thought about it I realised you haven't been yourself recently.'

'Sholto?' Tara's eyes fixed on her friend. 'Is he all right?'

'Don't you two talk?'

'We're divorced,' Tara reminded her, looking down at the muffin she was clutching. It broke in her fingers, crumbling onto the plate. 'I haven't seen him for ages.' Weeks, crawling along day by day. When would she ever be really over him?

'He's okay, I guess,' Chantelle said. 'But I think Averil's death hit him pretty hard. He doesn't show his feelings much, does he? Very stiff upper lip. Only...just occasionally I catch a look in his eyes that makes me want to weep.'

Tara determinedly blinked tears from her own eyes. 'It takes time,' she said tritely.

'Apparently he has no family of his own.' Chantelle looked at Tara as if for confirmation.

Tara nodded. When her mother died, and then her father, her friends had tried their awkward best to sympathise, but none had been through what she was suffering. Sholto had said simply, 'I was a teenager when both my parents died.' And she'd known that here was someone who understood, although he was one of the few who hadn't said, 'I know how you must feel.'

Chantelle said, 'Mm, well, he and Averil's family are quite close now. Her parents think of him as a son-in-law, I guess. Anyway,' she added, 'how about the picnic? Can I put your name on the helpers' list?'

'Yes, of course, and I'll donate some prizes.' The children's picnic was an annual event, organised by Chantelle

and supported by nearly all the shopkeepers in the mall.
A nearby juvenile home housed children whose parents
were divorced or abusive, or for some reason unable or
unwilling to provide for them, either temporarily or permanently. The picnic was one way the shopkeepers and
their families helped.

A HIRED BUS and a small fleet of cars transported the
children, two of their carers, food and volunteer helpers
to the beach park not far from Auckland. Once there the
children tumbled gleefully out onto the grass, and the
helpers began unloading equipment and food and trying
to contain their charges in an area where they would be
under watchful eyes at all times.

Andy had brought Jane along, and Tara was passing
out ice-blocks to eager young hands when she looked up
and nearly dropped one. Sholto was standing not five feet
away, holding a carton of potato crisps.

'Hey!' a penetrating, childish voice said. 'Can I have
an ice-block, please?'

She handed it to him, then automatically dipped into
the insulated container for another. When she next
looked up Sholto had moved away.

Later he was helping to mark out a course for the children's races, and she spotted him again with a group of
boys entering the water for a swim. Most of the adults
had been allocated four youngsters who were their responsibility, especially in or near the water, and she was
astonished to see him letting the children ride on his
shoulders and tossing them into the water, a game they
never seemed to tire of. She even heard him laugh, and
watched in disbelief as they ganged up on him and he
pretended to be overwhelmed by their superior strength,
submitting to a ducking.

He surfaced, shook them off and grinned. 'But remember,' he said, his compelling voice carrying over the
short stretch of water, 'never do that to anyone who's
smaller than you, or afraid. Promise me!'

'Promise,' three voices chorused.

'Why?' demanded a stocky little Maori boy.

'Because it's mean and cruel, and it can be dangerous. Anyway, only cowards are cruel to other people.'

The boy looked unconvinced. He turned and started to show off an inelegant butterfly stroke. After lunch, she saw him go off along the beach with the other boys and Sholto, and watched as he placed his hand into the man's, looking up at him with a confiding air.

'Sholto's good with them,' Chantelle said, coming to Tara's side.

'You didn't tell me he would be here,' Tara accused her.

'Didn't know,' Chantelle answered tranquilly. 'Phil mentioned it to him last night, and he asked if we needed more helpers. Phil said—quite rightly—that we never turn down a volunteer.'

Had Phil mentioned that Tara would be attending? Probably not.

Chantelle said thoughtfully, 'Averil's brothers and sisters all have children. I remember her saying they brought out a different side of Sholto. He seems to be one of those buttoned-up people who only relax with kids.'

The children lined up for running races, three-legged races, sack races, and less competitive games where everyone got a prize.

The adults ran races, too, first the women, then the men.

Tara, beaten marginally by a racehorse-thin house mother from the home, while Jane huffed in last, subsided, panting, on the grass and watched Sholto, urged on by his junior cohort, resignedly shed his shoes and line up with the other men amid laughter and cheers.

He won easily, even Andy trailing behind, and accepted his prize of a plastic whistle and the proud congratulations of his small team of supporters with all solemnity before strolling over to lounge on the grass by Tara.

'Congratulations,' she said.

'Thanks.' He turned to the boys who had followed adoringly after him. 'Hey, fellers, do me a favour and fetch my shoes for me, would you?'

They ran off immediately, jostling each other in their eagerness to be first.

'Don't you have a bunch of kids to look after?' he asked her.

'Over there.' Tara nodded to where four youngsters wearing sand-encrusted T-shirts were happily building a lopsided castle.

Sholto glanced at them and looked back at Tara. She thought he was about to say something to her, but Andy and Jane, a gaggle of children surrounding them, strolled up hand in hand, and stopped to chat. Jane lifted her free hand to wave at someone, and catching the glint of diamonds, Tara asked, 'Is that an engagement ring?'

Jane exchanged a sheepish, secretly delighted look with Andy, and he grinned like a particularly proud Cheshire cat. 'Bought it yesterday,' he said. 'We're getting married after Christmas.'

Knowing what was expected of her, Tara jumped to her feet, gave them each a hug and congratulated them. If she had some misgivings, she was determined to hide them.

Sholto also got to his feet and added his best wishes. One of the children tugged at Jane's hand and led them away just as Sholto's group scampered back, with the outspoken little Maori boy in front, triumphantly clutching Sholto's shoes.

Sholto slipped into them. 'Look at that sandcastle over there.' He pointed. 'Pretty impressive, isn't it? Think you guys can do better?'

'Better than girls?' a freckled child said with scorn. ''Course we can!'

'There goes a budding male chauvinist,' Sholto murmured as he watched the boys scamper across the sand after each other.

'You seem to have some influence with them,' Tara replied. 'Use it.'

He cast her a slightly mocking glance, almost a smile. 'I may, later,' he promised. 'Meantime I'm glad of a breather. They use a lot of energy, kids.'

'I never realised that you liked children.'

He said after a moment, 'Until recently I hadn't had much to do with them.'

'You seem to cope very successfully. Some of these kids are pretty tough. They're not always easy to deal with.'

'They're all damaged, but hiding it. Aggression, competitiveness, accusations, it's all good cover.' He looked down and picked a blade of grass, idly splitting it.

'That's rather... perceptive of you.' Tara hesitated, then asked, 'Do you speak from experience?' Would he admit to her anything of what she now knew about his background?

Sholto's eyes briefly and searingly met hers. His mouth hardened as he looked out at the glittering water. 'Yes.'

After the single affirmative, his teeth clamped.

'I'm sorry,' she said, her voice very low.

He shrugged. 'I survived. These kids will, too.' Catching her shocked look, he added, 'I'm not saying they shouldn't have help.'

'Did you?'

'Not much.' He stirred and rose to his feet. 'It looks like another contretemps is developing over the sandcastle project. I'd better go and sort it out.'

Tara went to check on her charges' effort, admiring it extravagantly and helping with the finishing touches of shells and seaweed. By the time she'd finished, Sholto's group were dragging him off for some cliff climbing.

When it was time to pack and go home, the children went readily enough. Most of them looked tired but happy, and they were all replete with unaccustomed junk food and a surfeit of sand, sun and exercise.

Tara and Chantelle had arrived in the bus while Philip brought his car loaded with cartons of food, but

Chantelle had arranged for other volunteers to accompany the children and their supervisors on the way back. 'One way is enough to ask of anyone,' she averred with cheerful cynicism. 'I did the double trip once with the little darlings, and never again. I was deaf for days.' Tara was to go home with her in Philip's car. She didn't realise until they were getting into the car that Philip had brought Sholto along, and that they were all travelling back together.

'Go straight to your place, Phil,' Sholto suggested. 'I'll pick up my car there and drive Tara home. Save you the extra trip.'

Tara wanted to protest, but it made logical sense, and she bit her tongue. Ten minutes alone with Sholto in his car wouldn't kill her, and he sounded as though it wasn't a problem for him.

The transfer was made quickly, both Sholto and Tara declining to come in for a drink with Philip and Chantelle.

For the first five minutes of the journey neither of them spoke. Then, as he slowed for a traffic light, Sholto said, not looking at her, 'How fond are you of Andy Whatsisname?'

'Very,' she said. 'But I'm not in love with him, if that's what you mean.'

'You weren't thrilled at the engagement.'

He had noticed her split-second hesitation before she'd congratulated them. 'I have a small reservation, that's all,' she said coolly. 'I'd hate to see Andy hurt.'

'Jane seems a pleasant sort of person to me.'

'She's very pleasant. She's also a professor at the university.'

Sholto glanced at her, his lips pursed slightly as though he might have whistled. 'I see the problem.'

'Andy isn't stupid,' she said, 'but he thinks he is. I just hope Jane's friends don't reinforce the notion.'

'You wouldn't think they'd have much in common.'

'They both like the same music.'

'So did we.' He glanced at her again. 'It isn't enough, is it?'

'They have other things going for them.'

'Like—?'

Tara wondered if he was really interested or just making conversation. 'Andy's one of the nicest people I know.'

'And I'm not.' He was looking at the road ahead, his face betraying nothing.

'I wasn't talking about us,' Tara said. After a short pause she went on, 'But I wasn't very nice, either, at times. Jealousy is a nasty emotion.'

Sholto went on driving in silence as though he hadn't heard.

He didn't want to discuss their marriage, Tara thought tiredly. He was probably wise. What point was there in reopening old wounds? He had moved beyond that period of his life, closed the door on it. Sholto would never indulge in vain regrets about the past.

Then he said, rather carefully, as if he'd been thinking the words out, 'You're right. I shouldn't have allowed it to wreck our marriage.'

Regrets? Sholto was expressing regret? Tara hastily beat down an unwarranted leap of hope. 'We both made mistakes.'

He said, measuring the words, 'I... wasn't having an affair with Janette.'

'I know.' She saw his quick, incredulous glance and said, 'I guess it's far too late, but I know you weren't. I'm sorry I was so stupid about it at the time.'

He turned into her street and drew up outside her house before he spoke again. With the engine still running, he said, 'What made you change your mind?'

'Growing up,' she owned frankly. 'And... thinking about things.'

'You still seemed convinced of my guilt when we met at Chantelle's party.'

'Believing it had become a habit by then. And...I suppose I wanted it to be true, because if it wasn't, then I'd lost you over something that never happened.'

Sholto half-turned in his seat so that he was facing her. His hand went to the key and he switched off the engine. The silence seemed very loud. 'You told me,' he said slowly, 'that nothing had...taken place...between you and Derek.' She saw his chest heave deeply. One hand was still on the steering wheel, holding tight. 'Was that true, or were you just frightened into denying everything?'

Was that what he had thought, that she was too terrified to admit the truth? 'I asked him into the bedroom,' she admitted, her voice low and ashamed. 'We were intending to...to make love—' She faltered at the sound of his hissing, indrawn breath, but he hadn't moved. 'And then I changed my mind. I told Derek I couldn't go through with it after all. I told him he had to go.'

She'd let Derek gently slip her dress off as he kissed her and held her without overt passion. She'd deliberately shut out everything but the tenderness with which he'd surrounded her, but when he began to shed his own clothes cold reality had hit her like an icy shower. She couldn't do this, it was wrong, totally wrong.

'I can't!' she'd said in panic, and when Derek swiftly tried to take her in his arms again, she'd pulled away, crying, 'I can't! I should never have let you—' She looked at him in horror, aware that she'd led him on. 'Oh, God! Derek, I know it's unforgivable. But you've got to leave now! You have every right to hate me—I'm so *sorry!*' She'd backed from him, aghast at the unrestrained wanting in his face, afraid that it was too late to stop him, that he'd insist on her following through. 'Please—I made a mistake—'

But his face changed as she shrank from him, the glittery look of desire changing to compassion. 'Okay,' he said. 'It's okay, Tara.' He took her hands, even though his own were trembling. 'It's all right, I think I half-expected this, anyway.' He leaned forward to kiss her forehead as she looked at him with guilty distress in her eyes.

And that was how Sholto had found them.

'I wronged both of you,' she said, 'you and Derek. I didn't love him, not in that way, and I never even thought so. I was just intent on some puerile, tipsy revenge. And there wasn't even anything to revenge myself for. I'll never regret anything so much as I regret that, for as long as I live.'

Sholto still hadn't moved. She said, 'I don't suppose it means anything to you now, but I can't help hoping you believe me. I know it's no use asking you to understand.' As he remained still and silent, she tried to smile, rather shakily. 'You wouldn't listen to me then. Well, thank you for listening now. I . . . I'd better go in.'

She made to find the door handle, and Sholto reached across her to put his hand on it, but didn't open it. His voice deep and steady, he said, 'May I come with you?'

CHAPTER ELEVEN

SHE MADE them coffee while he waited for her in the living room. Carrying in the cups, she tried to extinguish the renewed flare of hope in her heart.

He drank his coffee in silence, and Tara sipped at hers, hardly tasting it. Sholto had taken a chair opposite her, but as soon as he'd finished his cup he stood up as though he couldn't remain sitting a moment longer. She was afraid he was going to go, but instead he wandered to the mantel and began fiddling with the ornaments on it—picking up and putting down the Wedgwood vase, tracing the pattern on the Indian brass tray with a fingertip, and lifting and replacing the lid of the Dresden china box.

When finally he started to speak, he still had his back to her, and at first his voice was so low she had to strain to hear it.

'I never told you exactly how my parents died,' he said. 'My father—' He stopped. 'He—'

'I know.' Her voice was very quiet. Perhaps she shouldn't interrupt, but this was obviously difficult for him. 'Derek told me,' she explained as he shot her a frowning, questioning glance. She hoped it wasn't the worst thing she could say.

When Sholto didn't volunteer any more, she added, 'He said that you blamed yourself, but he didn't know why.'

His shoulders moved, and she thought he wasn't going to reply, but then he said, apparently concentrating his attention on the empty fireplace and the fan-shaped firescreen before it, 'The night before, I'd squared up to him. Told him to leave my mother alone, or buy a fight with *me*. I was fifteen, and he was still bigger than me, but he was drunk and I think I might have stood a chance.'

Tara's breath caught. 'Did he hit you?'

He gave her a fleeting glance of mild surprise. 'He yelled a lot about teaching me a lesson and being boss in his own house, and threw a few wild punches that didn't do me any serious harm. But he didn't touch my mother. I thought I'd won—oh, I was very cocky. But the next day he came home from work early and...and nearly killed her. He did kill her—when he'd finished with her it was only a matter of time.'

Picking up the vase again, he half-turned towards her, but his eyes were on the raised Wedgwood pattern, his thumb gently rubbing over it, although she doubted if he was seeing it.

Tara said, 'It wasn't your fault that you couldn't protect your mother.'

'But I had to try,' he said on an acrid note of satire that at first puzzled her, 'didn't I? Had to be the little hero. And it only made things worse.' He turned and carefully replaced the vase. Staring at it, he said, 'Ever since I could remember, he'd been hitting her. For anything, everything. His meal wasn't on the table dead on six o'clock, or the potatoes were burnt, he couldn't find his clean shirts, there was a hole in his sock—and she always made excuses, explanations, tried to make him understand why she'd...failed this time. She never seemed to understand that it didn't do any good, that he was going to hit her anyway. Sometimes I got angry with *her* because she wouldn't see...she just kept on talking at him, trying to stave off the inevitable with excuses...endless, futile excuses.'

Tara sat biting her lip hard, trying to envisage what it must have been like for a child.

He said, 'I was nearly ten before I realised that other people didn't live like that, that Derek's father, for instance, wouldn't have dreamed of laying a hand on his wife. All I wanted, from that time on, was to grow big enough to give my dad back what he deserved and get my mother out.'

She wondered why he'd chosen suddenly to talk to her about it. Perhaps Averil's death had brought it back to him, and he needed to confide in someone?

'When I was twelve, I told my mother we should leave, that we could go away somewhere, she didn't have to stay and keep taking it. She put up all sorts of objections— what about my schooling, what could we live on, where could we go—but when I kept on at her she came up with what for her was the final, inescapable argument. He *loved* her, she said. She couldn't leave because he loved her.'

Tara couldn't help a small gasp of revulsion. Sholto turned again, his eyes briefly on her face before he thrust his hands into his pockets and transferred his gaze to the mellowed old rug he stood on. 'When I asked her what earthly reason she had to think that this brute, this *animal* we lived with had ever loved her, she said, "But Sholto, you know how sorry he is after he's lost his temper." *You know how sorry he is.* That's what she said. Because after he'd left her bruised and crying and stormed out of the house yelling how useless she was, he'd come back hours later and *apologise*. Say he was sorry, it wouldn't happen again. Almost grovel before her. It was nauseating.'

'Did she *believe* him?'

'She'd pretend to. She'd take him in her arms and kiss him as though he was the one who needed to be comforted. It made me physically sick. Sometimes I'd go outside and throw up in the garden.'

Tara swallowed. She felt sick herself.

'I'm not saying all this to make you sorry for me,' he said, looking at her fully at last.

'I know.' It wasn't a bid for sympathy. Sholto would never ask for that. 'You said once that you don't believe in forgiveness. You're telling me why.'

He was telling her why he hadn't let her explain what happened with Derek, why he gave no one a second chance, the reason he'd said he could never trust her again, couldn't forgive her.

'You don't believe that excuses or apologies mean anything,' she said. 'It's why you refused to defend yourself when I accused you of being unfaithful.'

He said, as though he hated the memory, 'I'd already done more explaining to you than to anyone in my entire life.'

About to dispute it, she paused. He'd told her why he'd been to Janette's place that evening she'd thought he was staying home. Given her the bare facts, but for him even that was a major compromise. 'I suppose you tried,' she conceded. She hadn't realised at the time how hard it was for him to feel required to justify his actions. 'Did you care whether I believed you or not?'

His eyes momentarily blazed. 'Why do you think I came home in the middle of the day? Did you think I was spying on you—that I *expected* to find you in bed with Derek?'

Tara flinched. It had never even occurred to her to wonder. Had he come home hoping to mend the cracks in their relationship? Only to be confronted with proof that it was irretrievably damaged.

But he wasn't waiting for her to reply. He said bitterly, 'Why the *hell* do you think I let you go with Derek that day!'

That made no sense. 'You *made* me go!'

'To get you away from me,' he muttered, looking at the rug again.

'Because you...cared for me?' Scepticism coloured her voice.

'With a blind, besotted passion!' He threw an angry glance at her. 'You must have known that. I tried not to smother you with it. I knew that I'd snatched you up when you weren't ready, when you were too young and innocent to know what marriage to me would mean. But from the minute I laid eyes on you I'd wanted you so much...'

Tara regarded him open-mouthed, but he was looking down again. For the first time in his life, probably, he was revealing his emotions—even if they were in the past—and he couldn't meet her eyes while he did it.

'I took advantage of you while you were vulnerable with grief, alone and needing someone to cling to. I rushed you into bed and then into marriage before you'd had time to recover and decide for yourself what you wanted.'

He pushed a hand through his hair. 'When you got restless and wanted some kind of social life, I told myself I had to let you stretch your wings. You were entitled to enjoy yourself like other young people. I just hoped if I was patient and allowed you your freedom you'd stay with me.'

'I didn't *want* my freedom! I wanted you to share things with me—friends, outings, just...the ordinary things in life. I *asked* you to come with me!'

'I know, it was sweet of you. But I don't dance, I had no social skills. Among your friends, I felt middle-aged.'

'You were still only in your twenties when we got married!'

'Just.' And of course he'd never had the kind of young man's life that they'd had. Thrown on his own resources at fifteen after a traumatic childhood, he'd turned to looking after his injured mother, earning his living, making his way in the world. It was all he knew. 'I didn't know how to have fun. I thought,' he said, bringing the words out laboriously, 'that I wouldn't fit in, that you'd be embarrassed. I suppose I was afraid you'd realise what a social misfit you'd married.'

Social misfit? *Sholto?* 'You can mix with anyone!' she said. 'You're one of the most socially skilled people I know!'

'Oh, at business cocktail parties, society functions,' he said dismissively. 'I taught myself to make the right superficial noises in the right places. But...' He shrugged, as if unable to elucidate further.

Dimly, Tara began to understand. He was no good at intimacy. A group of friends was more threatening to him than a gathering of successful businessmen and politicians.

'I didn't enjoy myself without you,' she said. 'But I was hurt that you wouldn't join me, and in the end I was going out just to spite you, to show you that I could have a good time even if you couldn't be bothered being there with me.'

A glimmer of understanding lit his eyes. 'And you punished me by mentioning all the men you met who admired you.'

'I'm not proud of that. They didn't interest me, but I wanted to make you take notice of me.'

'If it's any use, I found it excruciatingly painful.'

Tara winced. 'Oh, Sholto—I was so young! I wish you could for—'

'Forgive you?' His mouth twisted wryly. 'Don't worry about it. Even at the time I had some awareness of what you were doing. I didn't think *you* did, though.'

'Not really. It wasn't a conscious thing.' Did that make it any better, or had she been wilfully blind? 'Even with Derek—I'd had almost a bottle of champagne. It's no excuse but, sober, I'd never have done it.' She paused, reminded that they'd strayed off the point. 'You surely didn't think I was in love with Derek? That wasn't why you sent me away with him!'

Sholto shook his head. 'Don't you know—even now? I was terrified of him leaving you alone with me. You wouldn't have been safe. Derek knew.'

Tara swallowed. 'I didn't believe him.'

'You don't know what danger you were in.'

'From *you?*'

He said roughly, 'When I came home and found you...with Derek, I knew I was no different from my father.'

'Sholto!' Her voice was fierce, shocked. 'You would never—'

'*You don't know!*' He turned on her, making her subside into silence.

There was no sound but the uneven rasp of his breathing. 'Once, I nearly killed someone,' Sholto confessed, his voice low.

When he'd been a mere child, goaded by a bully. 'I still don't believe,' Tara said, looking at him, 'that you would ever hurt me. Or any woman.'

'At the time I wouldn't have put money on it. I've never felt about any woman the way I...did...about you.'

'Averil...'

'Averil was completely different.'

Tara's gaze dropped. She'd almost forgotten about his dead fiancée, the girl who had softened and humanised him, made him into a man who could frolic with children, a man who for the first time in his life had become part of a normal family, who had wanted a family of his own.

'You're still grieving for her,' she said, reminding herself of the brutal truth. Perhaps it was his grief that had made him willing to pour out his heart in this way. Maybe this examination of the past was a way of helping him face the future.

'Yes,' he said. His voice sinking so that she strained to hear the words, he added, 'But what I grieve for most is that I let her down. She trusted me and...when I was with you, I couldn't be trusted.'

Her head jerked up, her eyes startled. 'Sholto, while she was alive you only kissed me! Surely she would understand... a reflex, some leftover emotion from when we were married. It was nothing to feel guilty about.'

'*Listen!*'

He looked so grim and intense she was jolted into silence. He stared at the ceiling for a moment, then walked towards her until he stood much closer, his brooding gaze fixed on her as if he had decided this had to be said face to face, with no evasion.

'When I met you,' he began, 'I hadn't had a lot to do with women. The odd encounter, a passing infatuation, that's all.'

He was no ladies' man, Derek had said, contradicting Tara's picture of him as an experienced lover.

'I'd had no time for a real love affair,' Sholto continued.

'Please,' she said, 'don't stand over me, Sholto. Sit down.'

He hesitated, then sat beside her on the sofa, but not touching her. As if relieved to break the eye contact he'd been determinedly holding, he leaned forward, his hands clasped tightly between his parted knees. 'I fell for you so far and so fast it was like drowning.'

'Me, too,' Tara whispered.

'I'd spent my life establishing control—of my life, of my business, of my temper that I was afraid was like my father's. Of everything, I guess.' His shoulders moved as he breathed deeply. 'I knew that I mustn't try to control you. I'd seen my father's way of controlling my mother, and what a disaster that could be. I tried like hell to curb my illogical desire to lock you up somewhere with me and throw away the key.

'What I didn't realise was that a relationship takes more than *not* doing things. Not establishing dominance, not trying to clip your wings, not scaring you by letting you know how totally consuming my desire for you was. I wanted you so much the wanting threatened to swamp everything else in my life. Nothing seemed to matter except being with you. That time I took you to

Hong Kong I nearly bungled the deal because I couldn't concentrate. I kept picturing you waiting for me back at the hotel, or walking around without me, and I wanted to tell them all to go to hell, I had to be with my wife. It seemed such a bloody waste that you were only streets away and we weren't together. I never dared take you on another business trip.'

'You didn't think of telling me why?'

His shoulders hunched in some kind of acknowledgement. 'I know now, I should have explained at the time.'

'I wish you had! I thought—'

'You thought I was substituting Janette for you. God! I scarcely even *saw* Janette except as an office machine. I valued her for that. I've made her manager in Australia, now.' As if it had just occurred to him, he said, 'I suppose you were hurt that I didn't take you away with me again.'

She'd been very hurt. 'I might have understood,' she told him, 'if you'd given me reasons.'

He gave a jerky, reluctant nod. 'Maybe—deep down—I was afraid of your knowing how much power you had over me, over my emotions. But I told myself that in a good marriage there's no need to explain.'

'I'm not a mind-reader, Sholto.'

'I know. I just find it extraordinarily difficult to...express my feelings.'

She saw that even using a phrase like that was an effort for him. He looked as though he'd just bitten into something sour.

Smiling faintly, she said, 'Actually, you're doing rather well.'

'Thank you,' he said quite seriously. He braced himself again, sitting straighter, even turning towards her a little on the sofa, although his eyes were on his tightly clamped hands. 'Anyway,' he said, stopping to clear his throat, 'I knew there was no way you'd forget how I'd treated you. So I figured I had to put it behind me and get on with life as best I could. I met Averil last year and...'

Clenching her teeth hard, Tara made no sound.

'She was a very serene person, a kind woman. I liked her. She talked to me about her family—her brothers and sisters, nieces and nephews—and she took me home to meet them all. I was welcomed as I'd never been in my life. When I realised she was in love with me, I found it difficult to credit. How could she have fallen for a boor like me?'

Tara blinked at him, but he seemed utterly sincere.

'I mean, Averil was gentle and peaceful,' Sholto said, 'and so secure in the love of her family. She was totally non-threatening.'

'Non-threatening?' Tara repeated. It was an odd word to use.

'I wasn't ever in danger of losing my temper with her,' Sholto explained. 'I didn't have an overwhelming urge to drag her to bed and make love to her until she'd have to beg me to stop. I never wanted to knock a man's teeth down his throat because he'd looked at her. With her I was a normal, civilised human being. She made me feel— safe. And she wasn't unattractive. I found—' his eyes flickered almost shamefacedly to Tara's for just an instant '—I found that I quite liked making love with her.'

Tara fiercely checked a dart of sheer, unadulterated jealousy.

As if he wanted to hurry over that part, Sholto went on quickly, 'I'd told her about you and she didn't mind that I'd been married. I thought we could have a good life together.' Deliberately he loosened his fingers. Sitting back a little, he looked at Tara sideways. 'I hadn't counted on meeting you so soon after I'd proposed to her. And I most certainly hadn't counted on still feeling the same about you.'

'It made you angry.'

'Yes,' he agreed simply. 'I tried to blame you. Kept lashing out at you, even tried to hate you. But it wasn't you I was fighting, it was my own feelings, and I despised myself for them.'

He said, as though each word hurt, 'After I kissed you at Chantelle's party, I told myself you'd taken me by surprise, and resurrected an old...habit. I think I came to see you later in order to put myself to the test, to prove that I was strong enough to resist you, to break your power over me. But that night, and almost every time I got near you, I couldn't stop the...the *wanting*. I discovered that I was as weak, as despicable as any other man when I was around you—as capable of making feeble excuses, breaking promises, giving myself one more chance, and another and another. I started inventing pretexts to put myself back into situations where I knew I'd no hope of keeping a rein on my most primitive feelings. So I was a liar and a cheat, after all. Every squalid, rotten thing that you accused me of.'

'Years ago!' she protested. 'I didn't mean—'

'It wasn't true then,' he said. 'But it is—was—now. I was committed to Averil, and at the same time wanting you so much I could hardly see straight. Dreaming of you every night, and, God help me, thinking of your face and your mouth when...' He closed his eyes and leaned back on the sofa.

Guessing at the rest, Tara didn't ask him to complete the sentence.

After a while he said tiredly, 'Even today—I'm supposed to be mourning Averil, you'd think at least I'd be able to honour her memory. I know Phil took me along to the picnic hoping to take my mind off losing her, but when he mentioned that the mall retailers were organising it, I thought immediately, *Tara will be there, I'll see Tara.* From that moment I knew I couldn't stay away. It's been the same for months.'

He lapsed into silence again. Except for the tight, tortured line of his mouth she'd have wondered if he was asleep. 'Did Averil know?' she enquired softly.

Sholto's eyes opened. 'I think she knew something had gone wrong. The worst thing to bear about her death was my guilt and remorse. You see, I had decided that when she came back from that trip I was going to have to tell her I couldn't go through with our marriage.'

'Oh, Sholto!' Instinctively, Tara put out her hand and closed it over one of his.

'It wouldn't have been fair to her. I didn't think for a minute that you'd have me back,' he said. 'But how could I promise to forsake all others when every time I saw you I lusted for you?'

He turned her hand in his and held it in a hard grasp, looking down at her imprisoned fingers, a fierce frown on his face.

'Lust,' Tara repeated sadly. 'Is that what it is?'

His grip increased so much that her bones ached. The silence stretched. She could hear a distant hum of traffic, and the sound of a twig tapping intermittently on her bedroom window. A wind had sprung up while they talked. She must trim the hibiscus, a task she'd been putting off for weeks.

At last Sholto stirred. 'No,' he said, sitting up so that he could look into her eyes. 'No. It was...longing—it was...love. You know I love you, Tara. I'll always love you as long as I live. You have my heart and my soul. My body and my mind. Everything I am. That may not be much, and I don't suppose you want it. But once you did. Once you did, and if memory is all I have to live on for the rest of my life, then—' he swallowed as if it hurt him '—so be it. I should warn you, though, I don't think I can ever stop doing my damnedest to win you back. If you find that unwelcome, I'm sorry. If you tell me to go away, I'll try—'

Tara placed her free hand over his mouth. 'Stop,' she said. 'Sholto...' she gave him a shaky smile '...I never thought I'd say this, but I wish you'd stop talking—stop talking and kiss me!' She took her hand away and looked into his dazed eyes. 'Please?'

She began to lean towards him, and Sholto, whose sudden stillness had been stone-like, moved so quickly that she gasped, and gathered her into his arms, holding her against him as though he'd never let go. At the touch of her mouth on his he shuddered, and even as his lips opened hers he was pressing her down against the sofa cushions, one hand fumbling for the elasticised tie that confined her hair.

He hauled the band off and then lifted his mouth as his hands stilled. 'If a kiss was all you wanted,' he said unsteadily, 'you'd better tell me now. I'm not going to be able to stop later.'

She smiled at him. 'I don't want you to stop. But if you're planning more than a kiss, why don't you take me to bed?'

'If I can wait that long.' He grabbed her hands in his and pressed them to his mouth. 'Are you sure about this?'

'Are you? I'm all sandy, you know.'

'I don't give a damn. So am I.' Pulling her up with him, he said, 'Do you mind? I mean, if you want to shower or something...'

Tara shook her head, and her hair spilled about her shoulders. 'Later.' She kissed his chin and moved closer to him. 'Take me to bed, Sholto.'

He did, with no more words. He adored her with his body, and gave her everything of himself. And received from her all the love and passion that had been denied him for those barren years.

'I love you,' he said once, the confession torn hoarsely from his throat, and heard her echo the words back to him.

Later there would be time for talking, and next time the talking would come more easily to him. He had bared his soul for her, perhaps the hardest thing he had ever done. He had trusted her as he'd never trusted anyone. He loved her as he'd never loved anyone. For her he had broken all the self-imposed rules by which he'd lived—never explain, never excuse, never forgive or ask forgiveness.

He was no open book to anyone, this man of hers. But he was her man, and she had all their lives to learn to read him, and teach him to read her. Tonight, she thought, before she stopped thinking and gave herself over to the sweet sensations evoked by his hands and his mouth and his warm body moving against hers, tonight they had made a good second start.

FLYAWAY VACATION SWEEPSTAKES!

This month's destination:

Glamorous LAS VEGAS!

Are you the lucky person who will win a free trip to Las Vegas? Think how much fun it would be to visit world-famous casinos... to see star-studded shows...to enjoy round-the-clock action in the city that never sleeps!

The facing page contains two Official Entry Coupons, as does each of the other books you received this shipment. Complete and return all the entry coupons— **the more times you enter, the better your chances of winning!**

Then keep your fingers crossed, because you'll find out by August 15, 1995 if you're the winner! If you are, here's what you'll get:

- Round-trip airfare for two to exciting Las Vegas!
- 4 days/3 nights at a fabulous first-class hotel!
- $500.00 pocket money for meals and entertainment!

Remember: The more times you enter, the better your chances of winning!*

*NO PURCHASE OR OBLIGATION TO CONTINUE BEING A SUBSCRIBER NECESSARY TO ENTER. SEE REVERSE SIDE OF ANY ENTRY COUPON FOR ALTERNATIVE MEANS OF ENTRY.

VLV KAL

FLYAWAY VACATION

SWEEPSTAKES

OFFICIAL ENTRY COUPON

This entry must be received by: JULY 30, 1995
This month's winner will be notified by: AUGUST 15, 1995
Trip must be taken between: SEPTEMBER 30, 1995-SEPTEMBER 30, 1996

YES, I want to win a vacation for two in Las Vegas. I understand the prize includes round-trip airfare, first-class hotel and $500.00 spending money. Please let me know if I'm the winner!

Name_____

Address _____ Apt. _____

City   State/Prov.   Zip/Postal Code

Account #_____

Return entry with invoice in reply envelope.

© 1995 HARLEQUIN ENTERPRISES LTD.   CLV KAL

OFFICIAL RULES

FLYAWAY VACATION SWEEPSTAKES 3449

NO PURCHASE OR OBLIGATION NECESSARY

Three Harlequin Reader Service 1995 shipments will contain respectively, coupons for entry into three different prize drawings, one for a trip for two to San Francisco, another for a trip for two to Las Vegas and the third for a trip for two to Orlando, Florida. To enter any drawing using an Entry Coupon, simply complete and mail according to directions.

There is no obligation to continue using the Reader Service to enter and be eligible for any prize drawing. You may also enter any drawing by hand printing the words "Flyaway Vacation," your name and address on a 3"x5" card and the destination of the prize you wish that entry to be considered for (i.e., San Francisco trip, Las Vegas trip or Orlando trip). Send your 3"x5" entries via first-class mail (limit: one entry per envelope) to: Flyaway Vacation Sweepstakes 3449, c/o Prize Destination you wish that entry to be considered for, P.O. Box 1315, Buffalo, NY 14269-1315, USA or P.O. Box 610, Fort Erie, Ontario L2A 5X3, Canada.

To be eligible for the San Francisco trip, entries must be received by 5/30/95; for the Las Vegas trip, 7/30/95; and for the Orlando trip, 9/30/95.

Winners will be determined in random drawings conducted under the supervision of D.L. Blair, Inc., an independent judging organization whose decisions are final, from among all eligible entries received for that drawing. San Francisco trip prize includes round-trip airfare for two, 4-day/3-night weekend accommodations at a first-class hotel, and $500 in cash (trip must be taken between 7/30/95—7/30/96, approximate prize value—$3,500); Las Vegas trip includes round-trip airfare for two, 4-day/3-night weekend accommodations at a first-class hotel, and $500 in cash (trip must be taken between 9/30/95—9/30/96, approximate prize value—$3,500); Orlando trip includes round-trip airfare for two, 4-day/3-night weekend accommodations at a first-class hotel, and $500 in cash (trip must be taken between 11/30/95—11/30/96, approximate prize value—$3,500). All travelers must sign and return a Release of Liability prior to travel. Hotel accommodations and flights are subject to accommodation and schedule availability. Sweepstakes open to residents of the U.S. (except Puerto Rico) and Canada, 18 years of age or older. Employees and immediate family members of Harlequin Enterprises, Ltd., D.L. Blair, Inc., their affiliates, subsidiaries and all other agencies, entities and persons connected with the use, marketing or conduct of this sweepstakes are not eligible. Odds of winning a prize are dependent upon the number of eligible entries received for that drawing. Prize drawing and winner notification for each drawing will occur no later than 15 days after deadline for entry eligibility for that drawing. Limit: one prize to an individual, family or organization. All applicable laws and regulations apply. Sweepstakes offer void wherever prohibited by law. Any litigation within the province of Quebec respecting the conduct and awarding of the prizes in this sweepstakes must be submitted to the Regies des loteries et Courses du Quebec. In order to win a prize, residents of Canada will be required to correctly answer a time-limited arithmetical skill-testing question. Value of prizes are in U.S. currency.

Winners will be obligated to sign and return an Affidavit of Eligibility within 30 days of notification. In the event of noncompliance within this time period, prize may not be awarded. If any prize or prize notification is returned as undeliverable, that prize will not be awarded. By acceptance of a prize, winner consents to use of his/her name, photograph or other likeness for purposes of advertising, trade and promotion on behalf of Harlequin Enterprises, Ltd., without further compensation, unless prohibited by law.

For the names of prizewinners (available after 12/31/95), send a self-addressed, stamped envelope to: Flyaway Vacation Sweepstakes 3449 Winners, P.O. Box 4200, Blair, NE 68009.

RVC KAL